WRANGLING A TEXAS FIRECRACKER

Copyright © April 2024 by Katie Lane

All rights reserved. Except for use in any review, the reproduction or utilization of this work in whole or in part in any form by any electronic, mechanical or other means, now known or hereinafter invented, including xerography, photocopying and recording, or in any information storage or retrieval system, is forbidden without the written permission of the publisher.

This book is a work of fiction. Names, characters, places, and incidents are a product of the writer's imagination. All rights reserved. Scanning, uploading, and electronic sharing of this book without the permission of the author is unlawful piracy and theft. To obtain permission to excerpt portions of the text, please contact the author at *katie@katielanebooks.com*

Thank you for respecting this author's hard work and livelihood.

Cover Design and Interior Format
© KILLION GROUP INC.

Wrangling a TEXAS FIRECRACKER

HOLIDAY RANCH
THREE

KATIE LANE

*To Sienna Grace, my dark-haired firecracker.
Never lose your fire and sparkle, Baby Girl.*

Chapter One

Four hundred and fifty-three wooly sheep later, Liberty Lou Holiday was still wide awake.

She wanted to blame her sleeplessness on being in the country. After living in an apartment in downtown Houston for the last five years, she was used to the sounds of a big city: bustling traffic, carousing drunks, and blaring sirens. She was no longer used to the creaks and hums of the old farmhouse she had grown up in. Or the chirp and buzz of the insect band that had positioned itself beneath her open window. But the truth was that it wasn't the cricket quartet or the creaks of the old farmhouse keeping her awake.

To Liberty, sleep was a waste of time. She would much rather be answering emails, uploading photographs from the last wedding on the Holiday Sisters Events website, posting on their social media sites, and maybe even watching some TikTok for event ideas. Unfortunately, the Wi-Fi at the ranch had gone out that morning and the Wi-Fi company couldn't send someone out until the following week.

So here she was, staring at the Jonas Brothers poster on the ceiling of her childhood bedroom and counting an entire flock of sheep. Maybe that was her problem. As a cattle rancher's daughter, maybe she shouldn't be counting sheep. Maybe she should be counting cows.

Not that her father owned cows anymore. All the cattle had been sold to pay off the ranch's debt. It still hadn't been enough to save the Holiday Ranch from foreclosure.

A few weeks ago, Liberty had wanted to hog-tie the owner of Oleander Investments, the company who was foreclosing on the ranch, string him up in the old oak tree in the backyard, and take turns with her five sisters beating him with a piñata stick. But after she learned he was the sweet boy she'd gone to high school with, her temper had cooled.

Corbin Whitlock wasn't the type of person to kick a family out of their home. He probably didn't even know the Holiday Ranch was being foreclosed on. Oleander was a large company and things happened in a large company that bosses weren't always aware of. Holiday Sisters Events was a small business and there were still things that slipped past Liberty. Thankfully, she had her twin sister, Belle, to catch those little details.

Liberty was sure as soon as Corbin found out who the ranch belonged to, he would stop the foreclosure proceedings immediately. He'd had a crush on Liberty in high school. When she met with him tomorrow morning, she intended to be the charming head cheerleader, homecoming queen, and student council president of all his adolescent dreams.

That was if she didn't have big bags under her eyes from lack of sleep.

Maybe what she needed to get to sleep wasn't sheep as much as exercise.

Tossing back the covers, she sat up and reached for her old roper cowboy boots. The leather was so soft and worn they molded to her feet like a cozy pair of slippers. In Houston, she wore designer high heels that added a good four inches to her already tall five-foot-nine-inch height. But here on the ranch, there were no snobby socialites she needed to impress—no arrogant businessmen she needed to intimidate.

Not wanting to wake her mama, daddy, and Grandma Mimi, she decided to exit the house the same way she had as a teenager. But climbing out the two-story window and down from the elm tree had been much easier when she'd been younger. Or maybe what had been easier was doing it in jeans versus a skimpy tank top and a pair of baggy boxers. By the time she finally made it to the ground, she had bark scrapes on the back of her thighs and a splinter in her butt.

After picking out the splinter, she headed toward the barn that sat behind the house. It was the quintessential country barn—big and red with a hayloft over the wide double doors. Just looking at it brought back sweet memories of grooming beloved horses, playing with litters of kittens and baby farm animals, having secret sister meetings in the hayloft, and, recently, hosting two weddings.

It was still hard to believe that Sweetie and Cloe were married . . . and that Cloe was now pregnant with Liberty's first niece or nephew. Just the thought of a sweet little baby caused her heart to clench with longing, but she had never been one to wallow in self-pity so she doused the feeling with a good dose of logic. She didn't have time for marriage or kids. Her entire focus should be on turning Holiday Sisters Events into the most successful event-planning business in all of Texas. She and Belle were well on their way to making that dream come true. Their calendar was filled all the way until next year with weddings, anniversary and birthday parties, and business and holiday events.

Which was why it was so hard being here when she should be back in Houston working alongside Belle. But all six of the Holiday sisters had agreed to take a shift staying at the farmhouse to help their parents and grandmother unravel the mess their daddy had made of the ranch's finances and help them through the process of losing the land that had been in her family for generations. Sweetie and Cloe had taken their turns and now it was Liberty's. Instead of bellyaching about it, she needed to concentrate on doing everything she could to keep her family from losing their house too.

And this barn.

After putting together two weddings for her sisters, Liberty had come to realize what a gold mine the barn was. It was a perfect wedding venue. She'd had more than a few clients who had wanted a country-themed wedding and would have loved having their wedding and reception in a barn—even if it was over an hour away from Houston. But since barn venues were snatched up quickly, they'd had to settle for a hotel reception with bales of hay and country decorations.

But if Liberty could convince a sweet country boy to not foreclose on her family's ranch, her new brother-in-law, Rome Remington, would pay off the loan in exchange for the land and Holiday Ranch would stay in the family. Mama, Daddy, and Mimi would get to keep the house and barn.

A barn that would become extremely profitable if Liberty had anything to say about it.

As she stood there looking at the barn and thinking about how much money she could make on it, a soft breeze blew over her, bringing with it the familiar scent of Texas wildflowers.

While she'd been born in the middle of summer, springtime was her favorite time in Texas. The winds were mild and the humidity low with temperatures usually in the high seventies or low eighties. Everywhere you looked, wildflowers bloomed in a rainbow of colors. Being that it was late April, the bluebonnets were gone, but primrose, poppies, Indian paintbrush, and phlox were in full bloom. The moon hung in the clear night sky like a relaxing C and clusters of stars twinkled like sequins on a prom dress.

As much as she hated to admit it, Liberty had

missed home. She had missed the wide-open spaces and the scent of rich earth and cow manure. She had missed the sky that stretched from horizon to horizon without one building or billboard to block the view.

Making her way around the barn, she headed across the open pasture. She didn't pay attention to where she was going, but somehow her feet knew. Before long, she reached a cluster of oaks, mesquite, and cypress trees.

Cooper Springs had always been one of her favorite spots on the ranch. In the very center of the trees was a crystal-clear pool of water that held memories of picnics with her family, skinny-dipping with her sisters, and fishing with her daddy. The clear blue water looked magical with the moon and stars reflected in its surface.

She didn't hesitate to slip off her boots and dip her toes in.

The water was cold, but not too cold. After the long walk, it felt good on her sweaty feet. She knew it would feel just as good on her naked body. She stripped off her tank top and boxers and dove in. The shock of the cold water took her breath away and she came up gasping. Her gasp turned to a startled shriek when a deep voice spoke behind her.

"It shore takes your breath away, don't it, darlin'?"

She whirled to see a man treading water not more than ten feet away. It was too dark to see the features of his face. All she could make out was the dark outline of his broad shoulders and the golden-red tint of his slicked-back hair. Once she got over her surprise, annoyance set in.

"This is private property. You have exactly ten seconds to get gone or I'm calling the sheriff—who just happens to be my brother-in-law and lives right down that road."

There wasn't a speck of concern in his reply. Just humor. "I hate to doubt a lady, but I am a little curious about how you plan on calling your big bad sheriff brother-in-law. Because if my eyes didn't deceive me—and they rarely do when I'm truly focused on something—you aren't carrying a cellphone."

Most women would be a little intimidated about now. It was dark. He was a stranger. She was alone ... and naked. But Liberty wasn't most women. She had a drawer of first-place ribbons in both the breaststroke and the hundred-yard dash. She knew she could outswim and outrun this cocky man with both hands tied behind her back.

She stared him down. "I don't need a cellphone when I was voted loudest cheerleader ever to grace the halls of Wilder High. Leave now or I'll make sure people hear me scream in the next county."

He held up his hands, moonlight reflecting off a pair of extremely well developed biceps. "Now don't get all riled, darlin'. I'm not here to cause any trouble. I heard how pretty Cooper Springs is and had to see it for myself." He lowered his hands and continued to tread. "I also heard that this property no longer belongs to the Holidays. And I'm assuming you're a Holiday."

Damn, the townsfolk of Wilder. They never had known when to keep their big mouths shut. "Yes, I'm a Holiday and you've heard wrong. Possession is nine-tenths of the law. And as long as my family is still living on this ranch, these springs are ours."

"That's not quite how the law works, but I'm not here to argue over who does and does not own these springs." He glanced around. "There seems to be plenty of space for two insomniacs to enjoy a late-night swim. I'm Jesse Cates, by the way. A mediocre rodeo roper and a restless wanderlust."

"So, basically, you're a rodeo bum."

His teeth flashed. "Pretty much. And you are?" When she started to answer, he cut her off. "No, wait. Let me guess. You're one of the infamous Holiday sisters. Since I heard Sweetheart and Clover are married and you don't seem to have a husband in tow, I'm going to say you're either Liberty, Belle, Halloween, or Noelle. Since I also heard that Belle and Liberty live in Houston and Noelle in Dallas, I'm going to have to go with Halloween. Or Hallie, as I hear you prefer to be called. And I can't very well blame you. I love the holiday, but sure wouldn't want to be named after it."

Liberty didn't correct him. "It sounds like the townsfolk have been running off at the mouth."

"What can I say? I have a way of putting people at ease. It's my face. Red hair and freckles aren't what you'd call threatening. If you could see it, you wouldn't be at all worried about sharing your springs with Opie Taylor." He pleaded, "Come on. Let me stay. I give you my word I'll keep my distance. I just need to get rid of some pent-up energy."

Since Liberty knew all about having too much energy, she understood his dilemma. "Fine. But get too close and I swear I'll scream these trees down."

Again, his smile flashed. "I believe it." With only a slight hesitation, he dipped under the water and started to do laps. She joined him, but kept on her side of the springs.

He was a good swimmer. His strokes were strong and consistent. He easily kept ahead of her. Which made her swim faster. But just as she started to pass him, he moved ahead again. It wasn't a race, but it sure as hell felt like one. Liberty wasn't about to let him beat her or outlast her. Even though her lungs burned and her muscles had started to cramp, she swam like she was swimming for the gold. But every time she started to pull ahead, he caught up. She got the distinct feeling he was toying with her.

Which really annoyed her.

At the opposite shore, she stopped swimming and came up for air. He went only a few strokes farther before he too stopped. During the swim, they had gotten closer. Liberty realized it had more to do with her than with him. He had stayed on his side, while she had been the one who had edged over in his lane. This close, his shoulders looked even broader and his biceps even bigger. It was still too dark to see his features clearly, but she could tell he was handsome with a strong jaw and that cocky smile.

"I won," he said in his thick east Texas drawl.

"I wasn't racing," she lied.

"Sure you weren't."

It annoyed her that he read her so easily. "I wasn't. If I had been, you wouldn't stand a chance."

"Then let's go again." She started to decline, but he added, "Unless you're not up for the challenge."

Even though her lungs still burned and her muscles felt like they had been wrung through her great-grandmother's antique washing machine, Liberty had never been able to ignore a challenge. "Oh, I'm up for it. But a challenge isn't a challenge without a reward. Twenty bucks says I'll beat that cocky grin off your face. Unless that's too much for a rodeo bum."

The cocky grin got even bigger. "Actually, I was thinking more of a hundred."

She snorted. "As if you have a hundred."

He stared back at her, his eyes dark and intense. "In the pocket of my jeans lying right over there by that tree, darlin'."

She hadn't really given much thought to what he had on under the water. Knowing he was probably as naked as she was made a tingle of sexual awareness settle in the pit of her stomach. She tried not to notice the way water droplets clung to his naked shoulders or the way the muscles in those shoulders flexed as he treaded.

"Fine," she said. "A hundred it is."

"And you have a hundred with you?"

"Well, no. But I'm good for it."

"I'm not saying you aren't a woman of your word, but you can't bet something you don't have. I have a hundred so I can bet a hundred. What do you have?"

"I don't usually bring money with me when I go for midnight swims."

"Then you'll have to bet something else against my hundred."

"Like what?"

He hesitated for only a second before he spoke. "How about a kiss?"

Chapter Two

JESSE CATES HAD never been one to gamble on something that wasn't a sure bet. He hated to lose money almost as much as he hated to lose a challenge. Not that he didn't occasionally go with his gut. But most decisions he made were well calculated and thoroughly thought through. From the moment he had figured out who he was dealing with, he should have backed off and left Cooper Springs. This wasn't the time or the place to have a run-in with one of the Holidays . . . that would come later.

But for some reason, he hadn't been able to bring himself to leave. And now he was issuing a silly bet. All because there was something about Hallie Holiday that intrigued him.

It had nothing to do with her looks. As much as he had teased her about seeing her naked, he hadn't seen much. It wasn't until she was this close that he'd seen her beauty. She *was* a beauty. Even in the dark, he could tell she was the type of woman who would turn men's heads.

He just wasn't the type of man who had his head turned easily. And a lot of beautiful women had tried. But not one of those women had him taking a second look. External beauty had never mattered to him. He had learned the hard way that physical beauty could hide all kinds of ugliness.

So, no, it wasn't Hallie's looks that attracted him. It was her moxie.

Most women would have screamed and run for the hills when they'd discovered they were completely alone in a secluded spot with a complete stranger. Hallie had demanded he get off her property. There hadn't been one speck of fear in her voice. Not one. While that was stupid—he was a complete stranger, after all—it was also damn brave.

And she wasn't only brave and sassy. She was competitive.

She had hated him getting ahead of her. Each time he had, she'd pulled back in the lead. Even though his muscles and lungs had been burning like hell, he couldn't help prodding her on. Not because he wanted to win—he cared nothing about winning at any sport and never had—but because he had enjoyed the game.

Was still enjoying it.

He couldn't remember the last time he'd enjoyed something that didn't have to do with making money. Making money had always been his main thrill in life. Even with an overflowing bank account, he still loved a good deal.

A chance at a kiss from Hallie Holiday for the loss of a measly hundred was a damn good deal.

But he had to get her to agree first. And she

didn't look like a woman who was about to acquiesce. She looked a little pissed that he would even make the offer. He couldn't blame her. A stranger trying to steal a kiss wasn't very chivalrous. If Shirlene or Billy were there, they'd give him a good ear boxing. But it was just one kiss. He didn't intend to let it go any further—even if his body was prodding him otherwise and had been since she had popped up so close he could see the soft swells of her breasts.

"Just a simple kiss," he said. "And after we're both fully dressed." She continued to remain silent. He knew she was weighing her odds. It made him like her even more. She wasn't one to make rushed decisions. He gave her a moment to consider before he went in for the kill. "Unless you're worried about losing."

He couldn't see the color of her eyes, but he could read the hard glint of determination. He knew as well as he'd known that Texas real estate was going to go down this year that she would accept his offer. Her need to win was stronger than her hesitation at kissing a stranger.

"Fine," she said. "But if you lose, you leave and never set foot on Holiday land again. And I get the hundred."

He lifted his eyebrows. "You think quite a lot of your kisses, Hallie Holiday."

"They're worth quite a lot." A smirk tilted her full lips. "Not that you'll be finding out. Ready, set, go!" She dove under the water and took off across the springs before he even had a chance to blink.

He tried to catch up, but she had too large a lead and was too good of a swimmer. She reached the rock long before he did, and then kept right on swimming until she got to the shore. By the time he arrived, she had already collected her clothes and was heading through the trees.

He thought about going after her, but his clothes and truck were on the opposite side of the springs and he figured she really would call her sheriff brother-in-law if he busted out of the trees as naked as the day he was born. Besides, it was probably for the best.

He had a job to do. It sure as hell wasn't kissing the Holidays.

But that didn't stop him from dreaming about a defiant, naked woodland nymph that night and waking up with a major hard-on. He had just slipped his hand under the sheet to take care of the problem when needle-sharp claws sliced through the cotton material and into his hand. He sprang up like a jack-in-the-box, shielding his man parts from further attack.

"Taylor Swift, you daughter of Satan!"

His assailant crouched low at the foot of the bed with her devil blue eyes blazing and her back arched in warning. Before he could prepare himself, she launched another attack, her orange-striped body sailing through the air and attaching itself to his thigh.

He howled in pain. "You little witch!"

He wanted to grab the little fur ball by the

scruff of the neck and toss her right out the open trailer window. But Corbin would kill him if he hurt his treasured pet. So instead, he gritted his teeth and one by one carefully detached her tiny claws from his leg.

Once he was free, he lifted the kitten and glared into her evil eyes. "I'm warning you, Tay-Tay. I don't care how much my brother loves you. If you sink your claws into me again—or bite me with those razor-sharp teeth, or sleep in my Stetson and cover it with hair, or use my boots for scratching posts—I swear I'm going to drown you in the nearest creek."

The kitten didn't seem at all upset by the threat. In fact, she growled a low demon growl that sent a shiver down Jesse's spine. The cat really was the daughter of Satan, and no matter how many cat toys he brought her or how many treats he gave her, she had it out for him.

Something he wasn't used to. Females usually loved him.

Again, his mind brought up Hallie. She had been just as prickly as Tay-Tay and he couldn't help worrying that maybe he was losing his touch.

Carefully, he held the kitten away from him as he got out of bed. Not that anyone would call the saggy double mattress on the floor a bed. But Jesse had slept on worse. Or not slept. Sleep had never come easily to him. His mind didn't have a shut-off valve. He was constantly thinking about the next moneymaking deal. So it didn't much matter where he laid his head at night—his fancy high-rise apartment in Houston, his family's huge mission-style ranch house in Bramble, or this beat-up trailer here in Wilder.

And the trailer *was* beat up. The roof leaked, the windows had cracks, and the exterior was covered in rust.

Jesse felt right at home.

Some of his happiest childhood memories were living in a trailer similar to this one. Except that trailer had a yard filled with junk. Junk that had kept four runaway foster kids from going hungry. It was where Jesse had developed his bargaining skills. At nine years old, he had sold the townsfolk of Bramble everything from washing machines to rare Harley motorcycles. He was proud of the fact that he had helped feed his sisters and brother. Not that Mia, Addie, and Brody had been his actual sisters and brother at the time. It was only later, once Shirlene and Billy had adopted them, that they became a family.

The best family a man could ask for.

But that hadn't stopped Jesse from trying to find his blood family—his beautiful mama with her volatile temper and his degenerate daddy who had shown up on only rare occasions and didn't seem to care that his son was being physically abused. But Jesse's second-grade teacher had. She'd called social services and Jesse had suddenly found himself in foster care.

He hadn't been happy about it. Even though his mama was abusive, he'd loved the hell out of her. Once he was an adult, he'd gone in search of her. He'd hoped she would have gained some kind of remorse and as soon as she saw him start crying and begging his forgiveness. Instead, she'd just stared at him with disgust and said, "You always were the spitting image of your no-good daddy."

His no-good daddy had been just as happy to see him when he'd showed up at his door—no doubt because he had a wife. But one good thing had come out of his visit with his daddy. He'd found out he had a half brother and sister.

Because Corbin and Sunny had been pawned off on different family members all their life, it had taken Jesse a while to find them. While he hadn't met Sunny, who was studying art in Paris, he had spent the last few years getting to know Corbin. He discovered that blood *was* thicker than water. He and Corbin were two peas in a pod. They both loved to make money and were good at it. And they both were dealing with the pain of abusive childhoods. But unlike Jesse, Corbin hadn't found the perfect family to ease that pain. He was still trying to run from the neglect he'd suffered from his mama and daddy.

When he and Corbin first met, Jesse couldn't blame him for not trusting him. Jesse had had to work hard to earn his trust. He'd started out giving Corbin sound business advice that made him millions and then helped him get started in his own business: Oleander Investments. Corbin had slowly started to trust Jesse. First, with business decisions, and then, with personal ones. Which was how Jesse had ended up watching Corbin's new adopted kitten while he went to Paris to visit Sunny. And why Jesse was meeting with Hank Holiday this morning.

Being born and raised in Texas, Jesse knew talking with a tough Texas rancher about foreclosing on his ranch was going to be as much fun as cat-sitting Tay-Tay. But business was business and the conditions of the loans had been spelled out in detail. Hank Holiday knew the consequences of missing payments when he'd signed the contract and used his ranch for collateral.

After making sure Tay-Tay was fed and safely closed off in the spare room, Jesse showered—or tried to in the low water pressure—got dressed, and headed into town.

Wilder, Texas, reminded him a lot of his hometown of Bramble. The main street was a block long and only contained the most essential businesses: a gas station, hardware store, feedstore, bank, general store that sold everything from horse liniment to frozen pizza, barber shop and hair salon, bar that served damn good barbecue and had a dance floor half the size of a football field, and a café that he'd heard sold the best damn muffins in Texas.

He was about to find out.

But on the way to the café, he passed a large For Sale sign on the side of the road. Jesse had never been able to ignore a sale. He turned around and followed the arrow off the main road and along a tree-lined drive. At the end of the drive was an old antebellum mansion with huge columns and a balcony on the second floor. The house looked like it had been vacant for a long time. Most of the windows were broken and vines and foliage had taken over the lower level and grand entryway.

Still, it was a cool house.

He tried the doors, but they were locked so he walked around the property as his mind conjured up a picture of what the house had once been ... and could be again with a lot of work and money. But even if he were willing to spend the time and money to restore the old mansion and carriage house that sat behind it, what would he do with an antebellum house in Wilder, Texas?

He shook his head and went back to his truck.

He could more than afford a brand-new truck with all the bells and whistles. But while money meant a lot to him, material things didn't ... unless they had sentimental value. The old, jacked-up monster truck he drove had that in spades.

It had been Billy's—or Bubba's, as the townsfolk of Bramble called him—ever since Jesse had known him. When Jesse got back from the marines, Billy had given it to him. He hadn't owned another truck since and he never would. The truck meant too much to him. And people seemed to get a real kick out of seeing the lifted truck coming down the street with its big mud tires eating up the asphalt and the American and Texas flags waving from the poles attached to either side of the cab.

It made him a little famous wherever he went. Including Wilder.

"That's one badass truck," a big-bellied guy said as soon as Jesse stepped in the door of Nothin'

But Muffins. "I bet you could roll over fifty Kias with them tires."

Jesse grinned. "More like a hun-nerd."

"Shiiit," the man said. "I'd like to see that."

An old woman with bright red hair and a ratty-looking fur coat sat at the window table. "Who cares about how many cars a truck can roll over? What you should be wantin' to see, Coach Denny, is our high school football team winning another state championship. They flat-out sucked last season."

"Now, Ms. Stokes, it's not my fault the kids today just don't have the same talent as they used to."

"Don't blame it on the kids, Denny!" the woman behind the counter snapped. She was a big gal with a long black braid and full bosom that stretched out the words *Check out my muffins* printed across her pink T-shirt. "If a team loses, there's no one to blame but the coach."

Coach Denny's face turned bright red. "I've won two state championships!"

"That had nothing to do with you and everything to do with Jace Carson," Mrs. Stokes said before she started coughing like she was going to cough up a fur ball . . . or a lung.

Jesse moved closer. "You okay, ma'am?"

"Give her a minute." Coach Denny waited until the woman had finished coughing before he spoke. "Lord, I miss Jace."

"He'll be back," Mrs. Stokes said. "He was too much a part of this town to leave it forever."

"Let's hope so," the woman behind the counter said before she turned her attention to Jesse. "Can I help you?"

"Yes, ma'am. I heard this place makes the best muffins in Texas."

She beamed. "Then you heard right." She spread her arms over the display case. "Just pick your poison. I bake them fresh every mornin'."

He looked at the wide array of muffins from Cinnamon Monkey Swirl to Pea-Nutty Buddy. From Sour Lemon Poppy to Everything but the Kitchen Sink. It was a little overwhelming. "Any suggestions?"

The woman studied him intently. "You look like a Cocoa Java Junkie if ever I saw one."

He grinned. "You read my mind, darlin'."

Five minutes later, he was sitting at a table sipping the best cup of coffee he'd ever tasted and munching on a dark chocolate and coffee muffin that dreams were made of. Everyone in the café seemed to be watching him. He knew they were curious, but they didn't bombard him with questions. Instead, they just watched.

He finished off the muffin and wiped his mouth. "That was the best darn muffin I've ever had in my life."

Everyone grinned with pride as if they were the ones responsible.

"Damn straight," Coach Denny said. "No muffins beat Sheryl Ann's."

"You'll get no argument from me." Jesse got up and threw away his napkin and handed his cof fee mug back to Sheryl Ann. "Thank you, Sheryl Ann. Maybe tomorrow I'll try that Red Velvet Valentine."

"Tomorrow?" Mrs. Stokes said. "So you're staying around here?"

He knew she wanted details, but he'd heard the gossip around town about the evil Corbin Whitlock taking the Holidays' ranch and he figured it would be best for everyone if he kept his answers vague.

"Yes, ma'am." He tipped his hat and walked out the door. As he headed down the street to the bank where he was supposed to meet with Hank Holiday, he couldn't help glancing back over his shoulder. Everyone in the café was crowded in the window watching him. He smiled and waved.

God, he loved small towns.

Since he was a good fifteen minutes early, he figured he'd be the first one to arrive for the meeting. But when he stepped into the bank, the receptionist informed him that Mr. Holiday was waiting in the conference room.

At least that's what he'd thought she'd said. But when he got to the conference room, he didn't find a mean-looking rancher who had a bone to pick. He found a stunningly beautiful woman with long ebony hair and eyes the exact color of the dew-drenched meadows he'd seen in Ireland.

Jesse knew instantly that this was the woman he'd skinny-dipped with the night before. He didn't know how he knew it. He just did. He was struck speechless by her beauty and he had never been struck speechless in his life. While he stood there staring like an idiot, the receptionist made the introductions.

Two words snapped him out of his stunned daze.

Liberty Holiday.

Chapter Three

THE BRIGHT SMILE Liberty had pinned on her face faded when she saw the man who had followed the receptionist into the conference room reserved for the meeting. She had been expecting Corbin Whitlock. But unless Corbin had gotten reconstructive surgery, shrunk a few inches, and done a whole helluva lot of working out, this man wasn't Corbin.

Corbin had been cute with dark blond hair and soft blue eyes. There was nothing cute about this man. Rugged was the only word that came to mind. A slightly crooked nose sat in the middle of an angular face half covered in dark scruff. While Corbin had been skinny, this man had broad shoulders that filled the doorway and had a tingle of familiarity settling in her stomach.

She understood why when the receptionist made the introductions.

"Mr. Cates, this is Liberty Holiday. Ms. Holiday, Jesse Cates."

Jesse Cates?

Liberty stared at the man who had just swept off his Stetson. While his face was rugged, his hair was a hat-mussed mess of strawberry-blond waves. Beneath that crown of golden red were rich chocolate eyes that reminded Liberty of the Labrador she'd had as a kid—soulful with a spark of deviltry.

He stared at her for what felt like an eternity before a big smile spread over his face. Last night, all she'd been able to see was a flash of white teeth. Today, she could see the way his eyes crinkled at the corners and the ever-so-slight chip in the second tooth on the right side. Freckles were sprinkled over the bridge of a roman nose and high cheekbones. The chipped tooth, red hair, and freckles did make him look like Opie Taylor . . . the roman nose, square jaw, and deep-set eyes were more Hugh Jackman's Wolverine.

The mixture was extremely unsettling.

"It's a pleasure to meet you, Ms. Holiday." His eyes narrowed. "Although I have the distinct feeling I've met you before. You ever been to Bramble, Texas?"

Liberty was still too stunned by his presence to speak. It took the receptionist making her excuses and leaving before she snapped out of her confusion and jumped to her feet.

"Just what the hell do you think you're doing? Are you stalking me?"

His gaze swept over her from head to toe. Usually, she dressed in heels and a power suit for business meetings. Today, she had chosen to wear something a little more feminine and flirty. Her floral-print dress was short and formfitting, her cowboy boots high heeled and a flamboyant turquoise. When Jesse returned his gaze to hers, it was easy to read male appreciation. Which was exactly what she'd been shooting for . . . except with a completely different male.

A male who would be here any second.

"Never mind," she said. "I don't care what you're doing here. I just want you to leave. And now. I have an important business meeting and I don't need some rodeo bum screwing it up."

His gaze lowered again. "You always dress for business meetings like you're heading to a honky-tonk?"

Even though that was exactly how she looked, she didn't care for him pointing it out. "That's none of your damn business. Now get gone!" She pointed at the door.

He laughed. "You trying to get rid of me is becoming a little bit of a habit, don't you think, darlin'?"

"What's becomin' a habit, darlin', is you showing up in places you aren't welcome. And by the way, you owe me a hundred dollars."

His eyes widened. "Like hell I do. You cheated."

She sent him a smug look. "I said 'ready, set, go.' I can't help it if you weren't ready." She thought he'd get angry. Instead, he gave her another one of those blinding smiles . . . that if she was truthful, left her a little breathless.

"I'm always ready, darlin'. I'm just not always prepared. You took me by surprise. But I promise you, it won't happen again."

"You're right. Because you won't be showing

up at Cooper Springs again. Unless you're a man who doesn't honor his bets."

He studied her for a moment before he pulled his wallet out of his back pocket and flipped it open. There was a picture in the plastic cover where a driver's license usually went. A picture of a big family standing in front of a Christmas tree in matching candy-cane-striped pajamas. It was an odd thing for a rodeo bum to carry around in his wallet. Until Sweetie had gotten in a big fight with Daddy and refused to come home for Christmas, the Holidays had taken matching-pajama pictures every year—with Liberty organizing the pose, of course. Seeing the family photo made her feel a little less annoyed with the man.

As did the hundred-dollar bill he held out. "I'm a man of my word. I won't set foot on land owned by the Holidays again."

The way he worded his oath made her more than a little skeptical, but she didn't have time to argue the point. She took the money. "Thank you. Now get out of here before the man I'm meeting shows up."

He closed his wallet and slipped it back in his pocket. "So I take it your daddy isn't coming to the meeting?"

The question confused her. "Not that it's any of your business, but my daddy doesn't attend all my meetings."

"Even if they're about his ranch?"

She rolled her eyes. "Good Lord, this town just doesn't know when to keep their mouths shut.

They had no business talking to you about Holiday Ranch business."

He hesitated for only a moment before he spoke. "They didn't. Corbin did."

She stared at him. "Corbin?"

He nodded. "He would have been here, but he's in Paris. So he asked me to handle the meeting."

It took her moment to absorb what he was saying. "He asked you to handle the meeting? You work for him?"

He hesitated. "Sort of."

Things started to fall into place. Her mere annoyance shot to anger in the time it took to blink. "That's how you heard about Cooper Springs," she said. "You knew we no longer owned the ranch. You were there scoping out the land your boss is stealing from my family."

He held up his hands. "Now don't be getting all bent out of shape. I wasn't there scoping out your ranch. I really couldn't sleep and thought a swim might help."

"But you knew you were meeting with me today and you never said a word."

"Not you. Your father."

Her eyes narrowed. "Which makes your deception more acceptable? You should have told me who you were, instead of acting like you were some wanderlust rodeo cowboy who just wanted a midnight swim."

"I believe you weren't real honest about who you were either. But you're right. I should have told you who I was. I just didn't know how much your daddy had told you about the foreclosure.

Corbin thought this meeting was with Hank. Not one of his daughters."

She stared at him as his words sank in. "Corbin knows it's the Holiday Ranch his company is foreclosing on?"

Jesse hesitated a long time before he gave one brief nod.

With that nod, Liberty flopped down in her chair in stunned disbelief. "But I don't understand. Why would Corbin want to foreclose on my family's ranch? He went to school with Belle and me. He wrote me poems and gave me wildflowers."

"You dated Corbin?"

Corbin *had* asked her out. And she'd accepted. But then the guy she'd had a major crush on had asked her out on the same night and she'd played sick. Something she was very thankful Corbin didn't know about. "No. He was just a nice guy who had a crush on me. Obviously, I was wrong about the nice part."

"You weren't wrong. Corbin is a good guy. But he's also a good businessman. Your daddy knew what he was getting into. If he didn't pay off the loan, Oleander Investments would get to keep the title to his ranch."

"We tried to pay off the loan—with full interest, I might add—but your boss wouldn't let us."

Jesse stared at her. "Wait a second. Your daddy tried to pay the loan off?"

"Not my daddy. My sister's husband, Rome Remington." She snorted. "Something I'm sure you already know. I wouldn't be surprised if you weren't the one behind the foreclosing. Don't all rodeo cowboys dream of owning their own ranch? Is that why you were sniffing around Cooper Springs last night? You were checking out your new home?"

"I'm not in the market for a home. Like I said before, I have a hard time staying in one place. But I would like to hear more about Rome paying off the loan."

There was a look of confusion in his eyes. She wanted to believe that he didn't know about Rome's offer. But after he didn't tell her who he was at Cooper Springs, she didn't trust him.

"The only person I'm willing to talk to is Corbin," she said. "I want you to get him on the phone right now."

She thought he would come up with some excuse for why he couldn't do that, but instead, he pulled his cellphone out of his pocket and tapped the screen a few times before he held it out to her. It was a brand-new top-of-the line iPhone. She knew because she wanted one for herself, but couldn't afford it. It confirmed that he wasn't just an underling at Oleander Investments. He was a top-paid executive.

She jerked the phone from him and held it to her ear. It only rang twice before it went to voicemail. She was pissed, but she knew that showing her anger wasn't going to save her family's ranch. So she pushed her fury down deep and tried to keep her voice light and friendly.

"Hey, Corbin! This is your old high school buddy, Libby Holiday. Long time, no see, right?"

She glanced up to see Jesse watching her with a smile playing on his lips. She glared at him before she swiveled her chair toward the window. "Anyway, I was hopin' we could catch up ... and maybe discuss the little ol' loan my family took out with you. So give me a call back when you get a chance." She rattled off her cellphone number before she ended with a bright, "Talk to yew soon!"

She hung up and swiveled back around to find the smile on Jesse's face had gotten bigger.

"Good job of sucking up, Libby."

She got up and lifted her middle finger. "Ms. Holiday to you, asshole." She swept out of the room without a backward glance.

Once she was on her way to the ranch, she tried calling Belle. Her twin sister had a way of calming her down and putting things into perspective. But Belle didn't answer and Liberty remembered she had a meeting with new clients. Which made Liberty feel even more ticked off that she wasn't in Houston. Especially when it looked like her presence in Wilder wasn't doing any good.

She had been so positive she could talk Corbin out of foreclosing on the ranch. Now she wasn't so sure. He didn't seem to care that it was the family ranch of the girls he'd gone to school with. Where had the sweet poem-writing boy gone?

It was something she intended to find out.

When she got to the ranch, she found her mama on the porch taking down the Easter decorations.

Darla Holiday loved holidays, which was why she name all her daughters after them, and had always covered the house inside and out with upcoming holiday decorations. After Easter, the porch was usually decorated for Mother's Day with a wreath of spring flowers and every surface filled with all the childhood crafts the Holiday sisters had made for her and Mimi over the years. So Liberty was surprised to see the plastic bins overflowing with red, white, and blue bunting and stars and stripes decorations.

"Isn't it a little early to be decorating for Memorial Day and Fourth of July, Mama?"

Darla continued wrapping the ceramic bunnies in tissue paper. "I wanted you and Belle to have your decorations in case we aren't here." She glanced around at all the plastic bins. "We probably won't have room to put all this up in our next house. Who knows if we'll even have a porch?"

Since it was true, Liberty said nothing.

Darla stopped wrapping and studied her. "I guess the meeting with Corbin didn't go well."

Liberty's anger returned. "I didn't meet with Corbin. I guess he's in Paris. I met with an Oleander executive who claims Corbin knows exactly who he's foreclosing on."

Mama looked confused. "That doesn't sound like Corbin. He was always such an honest, hardworking boy. It was a shame he was shipped off to one family member after the other like some unwanted, flea-bitten dog. If his family were good folk, that would be one thing. But we all know his uncle was not a good man. Which was why your daddy had to fire him."

Liberty remembered Corbin's uncle and had

never liked him. Not only because he was sullen and gruff, but also because he always smelled like whiskey.

"Maybe that's why Corbin is foreclosing on the ranch," she said. "Maybe he's doing it to get revenge for Daddy firing his uncle."

"Maybe, but I got the feeling there was no love lost between him and his uncle. Dan Wheeler passed away a few years ago and Corbin didn't even come back for his funeral."

"Then I don't get it," Liberty said. "I don't understand why Corbin is refusing to let Rome pay off the loan."

"You didn't ask his employee?"

"Jesse acted like he didn't know anything about it. And maybe he doesn't. He didn't hesitate to call Corbin when I demanded to talk to him. It was almost like he wanted answers too."

The screen door swung open and Mimi stepped out in one of her wide-brimmed gardening hats. When she spoke, it was obvious she'd been eavesdropping on their conversation. "Then maybe this Jesse will be our savior."

Liberty snorted. "Jesse Cates? Obviously, you haven't met the man. I get the feeling if he was in a burning building, the only one he'd be concerned about saving is himself. A cockier cowboy I've never met."

"You're not a cowboy worth your salt if you don't have a little swagger." Mimi's eyes narrowed on Liberty. "And you're pretty cocky yourself, young lady. Don't tell me that you and this Jesse got into it."

"I'm certainly not going to be nice to a man who is working for the villain kicking my family out of their home."

Mama sighed. "So, in other words, you let your temper get the best of you, Liberty Lou."

"Well, what was I supposed to do, Mama? Kiss his butt?"

"Yes!" Mimi said. "If it keeps this land in our family, that's exactly what you should have done. It was what you were planning to do with Corbin. Now it looks like it's up to me to fix this mess you've made."

Liberty was scared of few things. Her grandmother getting involved in family business was one of them. She held up her hands.

"Oh, no, Mimi. The last time you thought something was up to you to fix, your granddaughters were offered up to the men of Wilder like mares at a livestock auction."

Instead of looking offended, Mimi just smiled. "And look how well that plan worked out. It got one of my granddaughters married to a Remington who can run this ranch the way it needs to be run."

Liberty wanted to argue, but she couldn't. Mimi's harebrained plan to give the ranch to a Remington if one of the two brothers could convince one of her granddaughters to marry them *was* the reason Rome and Cloe had married. Unfortunately, it hadn't worked out exactly as planned. The fake marriage had become anything but fake and Rome hadn't ended up with the Holiday Ranch.

Corbin Whitlock had stopped that.

"If we have a ranch for Rome to run," Liberty said. "And that's looking doubtful."

"Then you didn't pay close enough attention to the golden rule I taught you." Mimi tugged on her gardening gloves. "Never underestimate a Texas woman when she sets her mind on something."

Chapter Four

It was only after Liberty left the conference room that Jesse felt like he could breathe again. He had heard about women taking your breath away. He had just never experienced it.

Until now.

As soon as she'd laid those pretty Irish green eyes on him, he'd felt like he'd been bucked off a Brahman bull and then slammed by the same bull into a wall. The entire time she'd been there, he'd struggled to catch his breath. And he couldn't figure out why. He'd been all over the world and had dated a lot of beautiful women. But not one of them had stolen his breath.

And his wits.

With his lack of oxygen, he'd struggled to keep up with their conversation. Now that she was gone, his brain started functioning again. The first thing that popped into it was Liberty's comment about Corbin refusing to let Rome Remington pay off Hank Holiday's loan. Liberty had to have misunderstood. Corbin wouldn't refuse the loan being paid off in full with interest. That made no sense. Corbin liked making money as much as Jesse did.

Jesse lifted his cellphone. Instead of calling Corbin again, who, with the international time change, was probably sleeping, he called the lawyer working on the foreclosure case.

When he had invested in Oleander Investments, he had made it clear to his brother that he would be a silent partner. He would offer advice when Corbin asked, but other than that, he'd let Corbin run the business the way he saw fit. He had no plans to change that. He wouldn't keep his brother's trust by breaking his word and butting his nose into the business. But he also couldn't help being curious.

"Yes, I talked with Mr. Remington's lawyers about paying off the loan," Samantha Letts said. "But Mr. Whitlock told me to refuse their offer."

"Did Corbin say why?"

"No. He just said to continue with the foreclosure. But I'm assuming he has a good reason. Mr. Whitlock doesn't make any decision without doing his research."

It was the truth. Corbin was the most thorough person Jesse had ever met. He spent hours reading every word of legal documents and just as many hours writing them. While Jesse occasionally went with his gut and took a chance, Corbin didn't leave anything to chance. He researched every business decision he made and had all the details before he made a move.

So why had he loaned Hank Holiday the

money? At first Jesse had thought it was strictly a good business opportunity. Interest rates were high. Whether Hank paid the loan off or Corbin ended up owning the ranch, it was a win-win proposition. But now that he'd found out about Rome Remington offering to pay off the loan in full, Jesse wasn't so sure this was a business deal to Corbin. If money were the incentive, why wouldn't he just let Rome pay off the loan? Especially when land prices were down and selling the ranch was a greater financial risk. Not to mention the hassle and legalities it took to foreclose on a ranch.

The questions continued to plague Jesse for the rest of the day—most of which was spent at the trailer keeping an eye on the daughter of Satan while he answered emails and dealt with his own business ventures.

As much as he enjoyed searching for new ways to make money, he had to admit that the thrill of choosing a good investment—whether stocks, real estate, or businesses—had been fading in the last couple years. Of course, his joy in a lot of things had been fading. Rodeo roping had lost its appeal. Traveling wasn't as exciting, and he'd started to feel bored and antsy after only days of being in a new country.

His family wanted him to come back to Bramble and help with the family business. He did love the little town, but after only a few weeks there, he started feeling like something was missing. And he had never wanted to piggyback on his family's wealth. He liked making his own way in the world. He knew Corbin liked that too. Which is why he'd stayed out of his brother's business.

Until now.

Around five o'clock, he tried calling Corbin. When his call went to voicemail, he left a brief message before he got Tay-Tay her dinner. The vicious kitten attacked it like a lion on its prey and devoured every last water-soaked kibble. Jesse felt just as hungry. But since there wasn't a speck of human food in the trailer, he would have to head into town for his supper. He went to pick up Tay-Tay to put her in her room, but she hissed and spat at him. Since there was nothing in the trailer that she could harm, or that could harm her, he held up his hands.

"Have it your way." It wasn't until he went to climb into his truck and a furry blur of orange jumped in before him, that he realized Tay-Tay had slipped out of the trailer when he'd opened the door. "Oh, no, you don't. You aren't coming with me." He went to grab the kitten that was crouched next to the gas petal and received a hiss and a scratch for his trouble. He jerked his hand back and checked for blood. "Maybe you aren't Satan's daughter. Maybe you're Satan himself."

She sent him a narrow-eyed look before slipping under the bench seat. Since he wasn't about to blindly put his hand under there, he gave up and climbed in.

"Fine. You want to come along for the ride, come along. You just better not get carsick."

As soon as they were on the road, the kitten cautiously climbed out from under the seat. She crouched on the floorboard for about a mile before she made the leap to the seat. Another mile and she was digging her claws into his upholstery and scaling the seat like a rock climber. She sat on the back for the rest of the trip into Wilder, her blue eyes staring out at the road.

He had planned on eating barbecue at Bobby Jay's bar, but he wasn't about to leave Tay-Tay in his beloved truck unsupervised—he was already upset over the claw holes she'd put in his upholstery. So he decided to try the little taco truck that was parked in front of the town hall.

After he took his first bite of the delectable soft chicken tacos oozing with guacamole and sour cream, he knew he'd made the right choice. He even shared a few chicken shreds with the kitten—tossing them to her rather than losing a finger.

After dinner, he should have headed back to the trailer. He hadn't gotten much sleep the night before and he was tired. But thoughts of Corbin and the Holidays' loan had him heading in the opposite direction.

The sun was setting by the time he drove under the grand Austin stone entrance to the Holiday Ranch. The other night when he'd come to Cooper Springs, it had been too dark to see much. Now, he could see the spring wildflowers that bloomed in a profusion of colors on either side of the road. It was beautiful, but the lack of cattle or horses meandering through those flowered fields proved that the ranch had fallen on hard times.

After passing the turnoff for Cooper Springs,

Jesse drove another mile and got his first glimpse of the house. The two-story farmhouse was painted a soft green with crisp white shutters and trim. A big ol' porch covered the entire front of the house, complete with cozy furniture and a swing. Mature trees grew on either side, their new spring leaves matching the green of the house.

Behind the house stood a towering red barn—the kind of barn that would make even a city slicker think of lazy summer days in the country.

Jesse slowed down and came to a stop, his gaze taking in the barn and the house and the porch and the rope swing that hung from a big old oak tree.

One word popped into his head.

Home.

A lump formed in Jesse's throat. For the first nine years of his life, he'd known what it felt like to be the kid standing out in the cold peering into the glass window of other people's homes. Homes with loving parents and a safe place to lay your head. Sometimes, he still felt like that kid looking in . . . he still felt like the little boy his own mother couldn't love.

He was so lost in thought that the loud rap on the window almost caused him to pee his Wranglers. Even Tay-Tay released a startled yowl and dove under the seat. He looked at the side window where the noise had come from, but he didn't see anyone. He had just started to think it had been an empty soda can or a tumbleweed that had blown into the truck when a gloved hand appeared and rapped on the window again.

He leaned over and rolled it down. "Hello?"

A snappish female voice drifted in. "Well, I'm certainly not going to talk to someone I can't see."

He opened his door and jumped down from the truck. He came around the front to see a little old woman in a wide-brimmed hat with a basket of wildflowers hooked over her arm. She wore scuffed roper boots, jeans with mud on the knees, and a shirt with two wild-eyed WWE wrestlers on the front.

He quickly took off his hat. "Sorry, ma'am. I didn't mean any disrespect. You just took me by surprise."

She stared at him from beneath the big brim. "And you think it's respectful to come on people's property and lurk around like some kind of criminal?"

He started to say he was lost, but for some reason, he couldn't bring himself to lie to a little old grandma. He figured this must be Mimi Holiday, Hank's mama. "No, ma'am. I've just heard a lot about the Holiday Ranch and I wanted to see it for myself."

He couldn't see her eyes in the shadow of the big hat, especially with the evening sun behind her, but he could feel her intense gaze. He knew she was trying to figure out who he was and what he was doing there. Before he could introduce himself—and, no doubt, tick her off—she figured it out on her own.

"You're that cocky cowboy my granddaughter

told me about. The one who works for Corbin Whitlock."

He had no doubt that Liberty had painted a dismal picture of him. "Not works exactly. We're more friends." He hated to lie to a grandma, but he also didn't want to be run out of town on a rail. Which is exactly what would happen if the townsfolk discovered he was not only related to Corbin, but also owned a piece of the company kicking the Holidays off their ranch. He figured it would be better for everyone if he just pretended to be a harmless friend. "I'm not here to cause any trouble. Like I said, I just wanted to see the ranch."

She hesitated for only a moment before she spoke. "Well, you can't see it from clear out here. Follow me back to the house and I'll give you a tour."

"Thank you, ma'am, but after our meeting today, I'm not sure your granddaughter will welcome me." That was an understatement.

"It's my name on the deed of this ranch. If I say you're welcome, you're welcome. Now come on." She waved a gloved hand and then headed across the pasture with her flower basket swinging at her side.

Jesse would have stopped her and made his excuses if he hadn't been so stunned. Mimi Holiday owned the ranch? Not Hank? Did Corbin know that? Since he thoroughly read all contracts, he would have to. There was no way Hank could have gotten a loan using the ranch as collateral if his mother hadn't signed off on it.

Corbin was taking a sweet little ol' grandma's home?

Jesse had straddled the line of what some folks would think was unscrupulous business behavior a few times in his life, but he had never kicked a grandma out of her house.

Nor could Jesse ignore a grandma's wishes.

He got back in his truck and drove toward the house.

It was even homier up close . . . and decorated like a float in a Fourth of July parade. American flags lined the walkway. Red, white, and blue bunting hung along the eaves. And a star-spangled wreath hung on the door. As soon as Jesse got down from the truck, that door flew open and a big man with a shotgun stepped out.

"If you heard about me giving away my ranch to the first man to marry one of my daughters, you heard wrong."

Jesse might have questioned that crazy statement if the gun hadn't been pointed at him. He held up his hands. "I'm not here for one of your daughters. In fact, I'll just be on my—"

"Stop pointing that gun, Hank William!" Mimi yelled as she came across the pasture. "He's a guest. I invited him."

Hank lowered the gun and turned to his mother. "Don't tell me you're trying to marry off another one of our girls, Mama. I think two getting married is quite enough."

Mimi snorted. "Did you hear him? He's not here for the girls. He's a friend of Corbin Whitlock."

The shotgun pointed at him again.

Shit.

"What in the world is going on?" A woman who was a shorter and older version of Liberty stepped out to the porch. Her daughter followed right behind.

That morning, Liberty had looked like a honky-tonk angel in the flirty dress and high-heeled boots. This evening, she looked like a country sweetheart in a western shirt knotted at her waist that showed off a peek of soft stomach and a pair of cut-off jean shorts that showed off mile-long legs. She was barefoot and her raven-black hair was put up into some kind of messy bun that Jesse had the urge to take down and mess even more. Her green eyes narrowed on him and once again all the air left his lungs.

"Jesse Cates." The way she said his name wasn't welcoming. Her voice held disgusted annoyance. So why did his heart start thumping like a bass drum in a high school marching band after a touchdown?

"Is that all you have to say, Libby Lou?" Mimi shook her head. "Where are youngins' manners these day? Introduce everyone properly, Liberty Holiday. You're not too old to get swats from your granny."

Liberty rolled her eyes before she made the introductions. "Mama, Daddy, Mimi, this is Jesse Cates. He works for that lowdown snake Corbin Whitlock. Jesse, this is my mama, Darla, my daddy, Hank, and my grandmother, Mitzy."

"Mimi is fine," Mimi said.

Darla looked more than a little confused, but she recovered her manners quickly. "Well, isn't it nice that you dropped by, Mr. Cates."

"Just Jesse," he said.

"You can call me Darla." She glanced at her husband who was still pointing the shotgun at Jesse. "Put the gun away, honey. I'm sure Jesse isn't here to kick us out of our house." She looked back at him. "Are you?"

"No, ma'am. I didn't even plan to stop by." He glanced at Mimi and she took over the explanation.

"I found him sitting out on the road in his big ol' truck. He claimed he just wanted to see the ranch for himself. So I figured we should give him the full tour." She turned to Liberty. "Why don't you do that, Libby Lou, while your mama and I fix him some sweet tea?"

Liberty opened her mouth to no doubt refuse, but then closed it again. After only a slight hesitation, she came down the porch steps to stand in front of him. He wished she hadn't. His body was already acting a fool. Being surrounded by her scent didn't help. She smelled like she looked—a country mix of spring flowers and home cooking. When he took a deep breath, the longing that punched him in the gut almost doubled him over.

She didn't feel the same way.

Her eyes flashed like green fire as she spoke between her teeth. "I'd be delighted to show you around the ranch your boss is planning on stealing."

"Not boss," Mimi corrected. "Jesse says they're friends."

Liberty gave him another blazing look before she turned and headed for the barn. Her jean shorts had been cut off unevenly and one perfectly curved butt cheek peeked out with every long stride she took. His mouth went dry and his knees turned to water.

Lord have mercy.

A chuckle pulled him out of his butt-cheek trance and he glanced over to find Mimi watching him with a smirk on her thin lips.

"You better get goin', Jesse Cates. Liberty isn't the type of woman who likes to be kept waiting."

Chapter Five

The last thing Liberty wanted to do was spend more time with Jesse Cates. She knew what Mimi was trying to do. She was trying to suck up to Jesse in hopes he could talk Corbin out of foreclosing on the ranch. But like Liberty tried to explain to her grandmother that morning, Jesse was the type of man who cared only for himself.

She knew this because she had dated more than her fair share of men and had become a bit of a connoisseur of the male species. There were men like Sheriff Decker Carson and Rome Remington—hardworking men who cared for their families and their town. They took life seriously. Then there were men like Jesse Cates—fun-lovin' good ol' boys who cared only about themselves. Their only desire was to enjoy life to the fullest. They took nothing serious. Liberty's family losing the ranch didn't mean a hill of beans to men like Jesse. She wasn't about to suck up to a man like that.

As soon as she was inside the barn, she whirled

around with every intention of telling him just that.

Except he hadn't followed her.

She moved to the open door and looked out. He was bent over with his head stuck in the cab of his obnoxious redneck truck. It figured he would drive a macho monstrosity with tires as big as a Volkswagen's. Two huge flags drooped from poles attached to the cab. As far as she was concerned, Texas and American flags had no business hanging over the bed of a dirty old truck—a truck with faded, peeling stickers cluttering the back window and a dented, rusted bumper. One was of a little boy peeing on a Ford emblem and another was a Dallas Cowboys star. The others were too faded to read, but she could guess that they said something arrogant and obnoxious.

She tapped her bare foot as she waited for him to finish whatever he was doing.

What was he doing?

Whatever it was, it hadn't been easy. When he finally pulled his head out of the truck, his Stetson was missing and his hair stood on end. He was holding a jean jacket tightly to his chest. Why he had spent so long looking for a jacket, she had no idea. It had to be over eighty degrees outside. It wasn't until he started toward the barn that she noticed the jacket wiggling.

"What in the world do you have?" she asked as soon as he stepped into the barn.

"The daughter of Satan." He lowered the collar of the jean jacket and a furry little head popped out. The sweet blue eyes blinked at her and

Liberty's heart melted. Babies of any kind were Liberty's weakness.

"Aww, you sweet little thing." She reached out to pet the tiger-striped kitten and received a sharp nip for her troubles. She jerked her hand back.

"I tried to warn you," Jesse said. "Tay-Tay has a bit of an attitude problem."

"Tay-Tay? As in Taylor Swift?"

He shifted the kitten in his arms. "That would be the Tay."

"Let me guess. Melba Wadley suckered you into adopting her."

"I don't get suckered, but Corbin sure did."

"This cute kitten belongs to that asshole? No wonder she's feeling used and abused." She gingerly held out her hand, then pulled it back when the cat hissed.

Jesse laughed. He had one of those deep-chest laughs that made you smile even when you didn't want to. "Believe me, this cat isn't abused. One look at her collar should tell you that."

Liberty leaned closer to examine the pink rhinestone collar around the kitten's neck, then wished she hadn't.

Jesse smelled good. Real good. After selling scented candles in high school, she knew a best-selling scent when she smelled it. She could make a fortune on a candle that smelled like Jesse Cates. He smelled like a mixture of all her best-selling candles. Home Sweet Home, that had smelled like a cozy blanket straight out of the dryer. Into the Woods, that had an oaky, autumn scent. And Liberty's all-time-favorite candle, Toasted Marshmallow, that smelled of night air and toasty campfires.

"Is something wrong?"

Jesse's question made her realize she was leaning into him and inhaling like he was a bouquet of flowers. She jumped back and tried to act like she'd only been examining the cat's collar.

"Don't tell me those are real diamonds."

"No. But they are Swarovski crystals and cost a pretty penny. I was there when Corbin ordered it. You should see her food and water dishes. He loves spoiling the women in his life. Especially his sister."

Liberty only vaguely remembered his sister. "So if you're friends with Corbin, explain why he refused to let Rome pay off our loan."

"I don't know and I haven't been able to get ahold of him." He hesitated. "You said that Corbin had a crush on you. Did you maybe do something to hurt his feelings?"

The truce they'd been experiencing ended and her anger flared. "So you think I'm the reason Corbin is being such an asshole?"

"I just don't understand why he wouldn't let Rome pay off the loan. It's just smart business."

She snorted. "I thought you told Mimi you were friends with Corbin. Which is it? Are you friends or do you help him run his business?"

"I don't help him run his business. But I know enough about the loan business to know that getting your money back with interest is the better deal. So there must be another reason Corbin is foreclosing." He held up the kitten. "You think I could put her down in one of the stalls?"

There was a part of Liberty, the pissed part, that wanted to tell him to get gone. But there was another part of her, the logical part, that was wondering if maybe Mimi was right. Maybe there was a chance Jesse could be their ally. Especially if he was Corbin's friend—a close friend if he was cat-sitting for him. Jesse did seem just as confused with Corbin's decision as she was. If she could get him on her side, maybe he would be willing to stand up to Corbin for her family.

"This way." She turned and headed to the stalls at the back of the barn. She opened the gate of the first stall and allowed Jesse to enter before her.

The stall was small and felt even smaller with the bales of hay stacked in it. For her sisters' weddings, they had cleaned the barn and stalls from top to bottom, removing all the old moldy hay bales. But because she'd wanted the country look for Cloe's wedding, she had ordered fresh bales to place around the barn for decorations and wedding guests to sit on. With her dreams of turning this barn into a money-making venue, she had made sure to keep the bales and stack them in the empty stalls for later use.

The thought of all the weddings she could have here made her need to enlist Jesse's help even stronger. She watched as he carefully set the kitten-filled jacket on the ground. Tay-Tay sprang out of the pile of denim immediately and raced between two bales of hay.

Jesse sighed. "We'll never get her out of there

because I'm sure as hell not reaching a hand in to get her."

"Scared of a little kitty?" Liberty sat down on a bale of hay. "I thought a rodeo cowboy could tame any animal."

"That's not a kitty. She's Satan incarnate."

"She's probably just missing her owner. When is Corbin getting back?"

"I don't know." He took a seat on the bale across from hers, his soft brown-eyed gaze direct. "But I plan to talk to him before that and see what's going on."

"I hope you'll relay the information. And just for your information, him wanting to foreclose on the ranch has nothing to do with me."

"Are you sure? You can be a little prickly."

"Only with men who annoy me."

He laughed. "Exactly why do I annoy you, Libby Lou?"

"That right there, for one. I feel like you're always laughing at me. As if I'm one great big joke to you." Most men would have denied it. But she was learning that Jesse Cates wasn't most men.

"I can't deny it," he said. "I do get a real kick out of you."

She glared at him. "And just what is so funny?"

He studied her for a long moment before he spoke. "You're like one of those Screaming Whizzer fireworks. You know, the ones you get on Fourth of July that spin on the ground erratically and make everyone scatter like quail out of a thicket. Even though you're scared to death they're going to land on you and catch you on fire, you can't help laughing as you dodge out of their way. They're terrifying but make you smile all at the same time."

Liberty didn't know if she'd just been insulted or complimented.

He clarified with an annoying grin.

"In case you're wondering, that was a compliment. Screaming Whizzers were my favorite fireworks growing up. In high school, I once traded a 1957 Chevy truck for three cases of them. Something Billy wanted to bust my britches for."

"Who's Billy?"

"My adoptive daddy."

Liberty had known quite a few adopted people over the years. Most had great stories to tell about their adoptive parents, but there were a couple that hadn't had such a good experience. It sounded like Jesse was the latter.

"Did Billy bust your britches often?"

Jesse's eyebrows lifted. "Is that wrinkle of concern between your brows for me, darlin'?"

"Don't be an arrogant jerk. It was just a question."

"So you don't care that I was beaten on a regular basis as a kid?"

Her heart tightened at the thought of a child, any child, being beaten. Children were a gift. A gift some people would never experience. Therefore, they should be cherished.

No wonder Jesse was a drifter who only worried about himself. He'd spent his childhood in fear. She started to say she was sorry—not just for his horrible childhood, but also for being so judgmental of him—when he grinned.

"Just kiddin'. Billy and Shirlene never raised a hand to us and were the best adoptive parents a boy could ask for."

"You jerk!" She jumped up and shoved him. Most of his weight must have been on the back of the hay bale because it started to tip. She might not like him, but she didn't want him cracking open his head on the hard cement floor either. She quickly reached out and grabbed on to his shirt to keep him from falling. Unfortunately, she misjudged his weight and her strength because he pulled her right along with him.

He landed with a grunt on his back and she landed on top of him. Both their legs rested on the hay bale, which pushed their bodies even closer together. Liberty could feel the inhalation of his breath and the thumping of his heart. She could feel the hardness of his chest and every other hard muscle . . . including the one beneath his fly.

The feeling that shot through her completely took her by surprise. Successful professionals, elite Houston athletes, and wealthy business owners had pursued her, but not one of them had elicited a spark of sexual awareness. And yet, this arrogant rodeo-roping drifter had caused an entire case of Screaming Whizzers to go off inside her.

She lifted her head, hoping his cocky smile would remind her body exactly the type of man she was squashed against. But Jesse wasn't wearing a cocky smile. His lips were parted as if he was struggling to breathe and his soft brown eyes didn't hold a twinkle of devilish delight. Instead, they held steamy heat. Steamy heat that kicked up her sexual awareness to pure sexual need.

When Liberty needed something, she always went about getting it.

Chapter Six

AT THE FIRST touch of Liberty's lips, Jesse completely lost the tight reins he'd been holding on his desire and it raced through him like a calf out of a roping chute. He wanted this woman like he had never wanted a woman before in his life. He actually shook from the potent need that coursed through his veins when she deepened the kiss and offered him the sweet heat of her mouth.

She tasted like cinnamon and apples. It was comforting and at the same time hot as hell. He'd had his fair share of kisses, but none of them had made him feel like this. The other kisses had just been necessary foreplay. He'd enjoyed them, but could have easily done without them and gotten straight to the main event.

But this kiss . . . this kiss was different.

Yes, he wanted sex. Since seeing her shorts playing peekaboo with one curvy butt cheek, he'd been living with a semi hard-on. Now it was a straining full-out erection begging for release. Usually, his brain would be trying to figure out the fastest way to get the woman's clothes off and get that release.

But with Liberty, his brain wasn't working on that plan. It wasn't working at all. His mind was completely blank as he just enjoyed. Enjoyed the way her breasts felt snugged against his chest. Enjoyed the way her fingers felt threaded through his hair. Enjoyed the way her lips and tongue felt brushing his. He didn't care about what came next. All he cared about was this kiss.

This amazing, heart-stopping, mind-stealing kiss.

"When I asked you to show Jesse around, Libby Lou, this wasn't quite what I had in mind."

At her grandmother's words, Liberty pulled back and stared at him in stunned disbelief for a second before she scrambled off him and turned to Mimi, who was standing in the doorway of the stall with a knowing twinkle in her eyes and the same smirk she'd had before.

Jesse thought Liberty would start rambling off an explanation. He should have known better. Liberty wasn't a woman who made excuses.

"Then you should have shown him around yourself." She swept by her grandmother without one glance in his direction. When she was gone, Mimi shook her head.

"She's like a wild mustang, that one. Her daddy thinks she needs a man with a firm hand to tame her. I think she needs one with plenty of patience. Are you patient, Jesse Cates?"

Jesse had thought Hank had been teasing his mama when he made the comment about Mimi trying to marry off her granddaughters. Now Jesse realized it hadn't been a joke. He wanted to make it extremely clear that he wasn't in the market for a wife.

Pulling his legs off the hay bale, he got to his feet and dusted hay off his backside. "I've never thought mustangs should be tamed—just appreciated . . . from a distance."

She chuckled. "It didn't look to me like you were admiring from a distance."

Damn. He'd walked right into that one.

"You're right. And I had no business kissing your granddaughter when I'm just passing through town."

Mimi didn't seem to be fazed by his announcement. "I had no desire to settle down either when I met Dale Holiday. I just stopped into town for gas on my way to wherever life led me. It turned out that life was leading me here." She hesitated. "I didn't have much of a home growing up. When I saw this place, I knew I'd found one to live out my days. Although it looks like that's not going to be the case."

He was really starting to wish that his curiosity hadn't gotten the best of him. Instead of coming to Holiday Ranch, he should have gone back to the trailer and stayed put until Corbin returned. Now he was stuck right smack dab in the middle of this mess and needed to take a side.

Having lived without one, he knew the importance of home. Which was why he sympathized with the Holidays. This was their home and it sounded like it had been their home for a long time.

But Corbin was his blood brother—a brother who had just started to trust him. He couldn't see Corbin being happy if Jesse broke his word about staying out of Oleander business and promised the Holidays they could keep their house.

So he only nodded. "Homes are special places."

"You have one?"

"No. I'm not really a home kind of guy. I'm more the sleep wherever I can rest my boots type."

Mimi studied him. "Well, maybe you'll find a place you feel comfortable enough in to take off those boots. Now come on and I'll give you the rest of the tour." Her eyes twinkled. "Not that it will be as entertaining as when my granddaughter showed you around."

He cleared his throat. "Thank you, ma'am, but I should probably get going."

"Nonsense. Darla has already cut you a slice of apple pie and she makes the best pie in the county."

So that's why Liberty had tasted like cinnamon and apples. One of Jesse's favorite desserts of all time was apple pie so there was no way he could decline. But before he could accept the offer, a meow drew his attention. He'd forgotten all about Tay-Tay.

He got down on his hands and knees to search for her. She was wedged between two stacks of hay bales. Preparing himself for pain, he reached in. But before he could grab her, she shot out and headed for the open door.

For an older woman, Mimi was fast. She reached down and scooped the kitten into her arms before Tay-Tay could escape.

"Be careful," Jesse warned. "She bites and scratches."

Tay-Tay hissed to prove his point, but Mimi didn't pay it any attention as she tucked the kitten close. "Now you just calm down, little lady. There's no reason to be scared. Mimi's got you and she's not going to let anything happen to you."

The kitten seemed to understand because she settled against Mimi's bosom like she'd just found a home.

Mimi stroked her head as she looked at Jesse. "Well, come on. Your slice of pie will sit there for only so long before Liberty helps herself. That child never has been able to resist temptation." She smiled. "Of any kind."

Darla's apple pie turned out to be a temptation. After wolfing down one slice, Jesse couldn't help accepting another. Although no matter how good the pie was, it didn't come close to being as good as the kiss. Now every time he ate apple pie, he'd think of Liberty Holiday.

Which was why he'd come to a decision.

There would be no more kissing Liberty.

Even if she was an ebony-haired beauty who kissed like a fallen angel.

He glanced across the table where that angel sat. Her hair was no longer in a bun. It fell around her shoulders in inky waves. He remembered sliding his hand into those silky strands as she'd kissed him and loosening them from the bun. They had slipped through his fingers like expensive satin sheets.

"So did you tell Jesse about your event-planning business, Libby Lou?"

Mimi's question pulled him out of his hair fantasies. He should have known Liberty was a business owner. She was too stubborn to work for anyone and too competitive not to want to prove she could succeed on her own.

"There's nothing to tell." Her voice was clipped. "We plan events."

"Now, Libby," her mama said. "You don't just plan events. Holiday Sisters Events have planned weddings and parties for some of the most influential people in Texas."

Jesse lifted his eyebrows. "Really? Like who?"

She duplicated his eyebrow lift. "I doubt you'd know them."

"Liberty Holiday!" Darla scolded before she changed the subject. "So I hear you're a professional rodeo roper, Jesse."

"Actually, I'm an ex-professional roper. And it was really more of a hobby than a job."

"So what's your job?" Hank asked. "Taking people's homes away?" He sat at the head of the table and, like his daughter, was looking at Jesse as if he were a spider who had been, unwittingly, invited into the fly's parlor.

He cleared his throat. "No, sir. I buy and sell things."

"Like what?"

"Whatever I think I can make a profit on—stocks, land, businesses."

"Ranches," Liberty said.

He shook his head. "I haven't bought or sold any ranches."

"So you're a city boy?" Mimi asked.

"I was until I was nine. Then I moved to the country. My family doesn't own a ranch, but they have horses and plenty of dogs and cats. And Sherman. But he's more of a family member than a pet." He glanced over at Liberty to find her studying him intently. What was going on behind those pretty green eyes? Was she thinking about their kiss and regretting it? Or maybe she wasn't thinking about the kiss at all. Maybe she was thinking about something else entirely.

Why that bothered him, he didn't know. Maybe because the kiss was all he could seem to think about. He had expected her to be a demanding kisser who took what she wanted. But she hadn't taken as much as given.

"Sherman?" Mimi brought him back to the conversation. Tay-Tay was curled up on the older woman's lap and purring like the sweetest little kitty cat ever as Mimi stroked her back.

"Sherman is our pet pig," Jesse said.

"A pig?"

"He's actually my Aunt Hope's. But Shirlene—my mama—loves him so much that Hope is willing to share custody. Half the week, he lives at my parents' house. The other half, he lives with Aunt Hope and Uncle Colt. Although I think he prefers our house because Shirlene gives him chocolate."

"Your house?" Liberty studied him. "So you still live with your parents?"

"Just a slip of the tongue. Like I said before, I don't stay in one place too long."

"So you're leaving soon?" Darla asked.

"As soon as Corbin gets back."

Hank snorted with disgust and Jesse figured he'd overstayed his welcome.

"Thank y'all for the pie and hospitality, but I should be going." He got up and everyone followed suit.

"Well, it was lovely to meet you, Jesse," Darla said.

"The same, ma'am." He carried his dishes to the sink, then walked over to Mimi and held open his jean jacket for her to put Tay-Tay in. Neither female was having it.

Tay-Tay hissed and Mimi scowled. "Now you two aren't ever going to get along if you don't accept and love her for who she is. She might be feisty, but she's just as scared as you are." Mimi sent him a pointed look. "You need to remember that."

Jesse had the scratches and bite marks to prove otherwise, but he didn't argue the point. Instead, he pulled on the jean jacket—mostly for protection—and reached for the kitten. She yowled and hissed, but only succeeded in scratching him once before he tucked her into his arm. "Nice meeting you, Ms. Mimi."

"Nice meeting you, Jesse. You need to come

back for supper before you go. How's tomorrow night sound?"

He could tell by the looks on Liberty's and Hank's faces that the invitation wasn't being issued by all the Holidays. "Thank you, but—"

"No buts. We'll see you tomorrow around five," Darla said. "Why don't you show our guest out, Libby?"

Once on the porch, Liberty shot him a mean look.

Talk about feisty. But he couldn't help laughing.

"I'm not coming to dinner tomorrow. So you can get that scowl off your face."

It remained. But it turned out it wasn't about the dinner invitation.

"I hope you didn't get the wrong idea about the kiss," she said.

"And what idea would that be?"

"That I'm interested in you. The kiss had nothing to do with you."

He should have left it at that and hightailed it out of there. He had made up his mind that any further interaction with Liberty was a bad idea. But bad idea or not, he couldn't leave without knowing.

"What did it have to do with?"

"Believe me, I don't have a clue. You are not the type of man I'm attracted to."

That stung. "Really? And exactly what type of man lights your fire, Libby Lou?"

"Not you. That's for sure. And would you stop calling me that?"

"I can't help it. It just sorta, involuntarily, rolls off my tongue."

Her gaze flashed down to his mouth and her lips parted on a soft exhalation like she was having wicked thoughts about his tongue. When she lifted her gaze, her green eyes *were* lit with fire. A fire that completely incinerated him. He forgot all about the promise he made to himself to stay the hell away from Liberty Holiday. With the hand that wasn't cradling the daughter of Satan, he reached out and hooked his thumb into a belt loop on Liberty's jean shorts and tugged her closer.

"So I don't light your fire? 'Cause you look pretty hot right now, darlin'."

She hooked her arms over his shoulders, her fingers threading through the hair at the nape of his neck. A tremor ran through him. "You look pretty hot yourself, darlin'."

"Burning up," he whispered right before he lowered his head and kissed her. Just like before, his mind went blank and all he could do was feel. The softness of her lips. The welcoming heat of her mouth. The wicked brush of her tongue as it danced with his in a hot tango that left him breathless and wanting more.

But as mindless as she made him, he had enough sense left to realize he couldn't take more on the front porch with her entire family—including her shotgun-toting daddy—only feet away.

Still, it took every ounce of willpower he had to pull away from those lush lips.

They were both breathing like they'd just finished a marathon. He was sure his eyes looked as lust filled as hers did. Before he gave in to those eyes and kissed her again, he stepped back and tried to put things into perspective.

"Obviously, we both light each other's fires. But considering the business side of things, I don't think it would be a good idea to let that fire burn."

The lust drained right out of those green eyes and they narrowed. "Let that fire burn? Exactly what fire are you talking about? Because if you think I'd have sex with you, you have another think coming. We might have kissed a couple times, but don't you dare be thinkin' I want to roll around in the sheets with you, Rodeo Man. Whatever it was that just happened had nothing to do with attraction and everything to do with boredom."

Damn, the woman knew exactly what to say to piss him off. "Boredom?"

She smiled smugly. "Exactly. You were just a fun little distraction. A distraction I'm over. So run along, darlin'." She flapped a hand like she was swatting a fly away. "You've overstayed your welcome."

For a moment, he had to fight the overwhelming desire to pull her back into his arms and prove her wrong. But that would contradict his entire previous speech. So he turned and headed for his truck. Once he'd climbed in and settled Tay-Tay in the passenger's seat—with only one nip—he reached for the key in the ignition. But before he could start the engine, Liberty stepped out in front of the truck. With her green eyes blazing and her ebony hair blowing in the stiff breeze, she looked like a pissed-off banshee.

Damn, she turned him on.

"As soon as your friend gets back in town, you tell him Liberty Holiday is looking for him. And I always find what I'm looking for."

Chapter Seven

"So let me get this straight. This Jesse Cates said that Corbin knows it's our family's ranch he's foreclosing on?" Sweetie added another packet of sugar to her coffee. She appeared to have a sweet tooth this morning. She'd ordered two lemon poppy seed muffins and had already inhaled one.

Liberty was meeting Sweetie and Cloe that morning at the Nothin' But Muffins café for breakfast. Since it was a glorious spring morning, they had decided to sit at one of the outside picnic tables. That, and they didn't want people listening in on their conversation. Not that the townsfolk didn't already know all about the Holiday Ranch's troubles. Gossip had always spread like wildfire in Wilder. Since most of the folks inside the café were staring out the window at them, she figured they were hoping to read lips and get some more.

Liberty shot them an annoyed look before she returned her attention to the conversation. "That's what Jesse said. But I don't trust the man as far as I can throw him. So I'm not going to believe

Corbin doesn't know it's the Holiday Ranch he's foreclosing on until I talk to him myself."

"When does he get back?" Sweetie peeled back the wrapper of her second muffin and took a big bite. Obviously, being a newlywed made you hungry. Cloe was on her second muffin too. Although she was eating for two so it was understandable. Liberty had only ordered black coffee. She'd had another sleepless night . . . this time because of an annoying rodeo cowboy.

"Jesse isn't sure when Corbin will get back. Which is suspicious. If he and Corbin are friends, why wouldn't he know?"

"But why would he lie about that?" Cloe asked.

"Why would Corbin ask Jesse to do his dirty work? That doesn't make any sense either. A rodeo roper knows nothing about the loan business—although he claims he does."

"Did you Google him?" Sweetie asked.

"Of course. And all I found was his rodeo stats. Mediocre stats at best. And you should see his old truck." She rolled her eyes. "A bigger, mud-splattered redneck-mobile I've never seen in my life. And his sweat-stained, crumpled cowboy hat is just as bad. The thing has to be twenty years old if it's a day."

"So you're judging a man by his truck and hat?" Cloe sent her a disappointed look.

"It's not just his truck and hat. It's his attitude. He's this smug, cocky jerk who struts around like his crap don't stink." When Sweetie exchanged knowing looks with Cloe, Liberty glanced between her sisters. "What?"

Sweetie shrugged. "It just seems like you're rather taken with this Jesse."

"Taken? I'm certainly not taken with Jesse Cates."

"Then why were you kissing him in the barn?"

Liberty huffed. "Mimi! I should have known she couldn't keep a secret." She glanced at the people looking out the window. "I'd be surprised if the entire town doesn't know by now."

"Mimi wouldn't tell the town about that," Cloe said. "Just family. And I don't know why you'd want to keep that a secret from us? We're your sisters, Libby. You can tell us anything."

Sweetie polished off the muffin and sucked the lemon icing off her fingers. "Clo's right. The Holiday Secret Sisterhood took a vow a long time ago to never keep secrets from each other. So do you want to tell us what's really going on between you and Jesse?"

"Nothing is going on between us . . . except two random kisses."

Sweetie's eyebrows lifted. "Two?"

"We sort of kissed on the porch when he was leaving."

"That doesn't sound like nothing," Cloe said. "Or random. One kiss can be random, but two?"

"Okay, so we're physically attracted to each other. But it's not going anywhere. Not only because he's friends with the man who is trying to foreclose on our family's ranch, but also because I'm too busy running a business to get into a relationship right now. As soon as I talk to

Corbin and figure out what's going on, I intend to get back to that business."

"And Jesse didn't have any information on why Corbin is foreclosing?"

She shook her head. "He acted like he didn't. Which makes Mimi think that if we suck up to him, he just might convince Corbin to stop the foreclosure proceedings. But I'm not about to pretend to like the man when I don't."

"You liked him enough to kiss him," Sweetie pointed out with a smug grin.

"I've kissed a lot of boys I didn't particularly like. It's called letting your hormones get the best of you. Believe me, it won't happen again."

"It shouldn't," Cloe said. "If Jesse is friends with Corbin, you and him getting involved isn't a good idea. It already sounds like you've gotten off on the wrong foot with him. I agree with Mimi. He could be the answer to all our problems." She hesitated. "Which is why I think it would be better if you went back to Houston and let Sweetie or me deal with him."

Liberty should have taken her sister up on the offer without hesitation and thanked her lucky stars that she could get back to Houston. But there was one problem: it wasn't in her nature to quit. When she set a task or a goal for herself, she achieved it. And she had set the goal of making sure her parents and grandma got to keep their home and Rome and Cloe could buy the ranch so it stayed in the family.

She intended to achieve that goal.

"I'm staying," she said. "Not only is it my turn

to be here and help Mama, Daddy, and Mimi, but I was high school friends with Corbin. If he's going to listen to anyone in the family, it's going to be me. Not to mention that you shouldn't have the added stress when you're pregnant, Cloe."

"She does have a point," Sweetie said. "Stress isn't good for expecting women. I've been reading up on it." Both Cloe and Liberty stared at her with surprise and she blushed as she rested a hand on her stomach. "I'm pregnant."

There was a pang of pain and just a twinge of jealousy before Liberty jumped up from her side of the picnic table to join Cloe in hugging Sweetie.

"That's awesome news, Sweetie!"

"Our babies will be born only months apart," Cloe said.

"I know," Sweetie said. "They can be best friends."

Liberty loved the thought of her nieces or nephews being close friends. "I'm so happy for y'all. Now Belle and I can plan a double baby show—"

She cut off when Fiona Stokes stepped out of the café. The older woman was decked out like always in an expensive suit, hose, heels, and her ratty mink stole.

Liberty couldn't help but smile. She'd always admired Mrs. Stokes's style. Not just her clothes, but also the way she thumbed her nose at society. She was a woman who did what she wanted and made no apologies for it. Whether it was her smoking habit, how she spent her loads of money, or the way she went through men like a raccoon went through trash, Mrs. Stokes was her own woman.

Not to mention that she didn't have children and seemed quite happy.

"With the way your sisters are hugging on you," Mrs. Stokes said. "And the way you've been ordering two Sour Lemon Poppy muffins instead of your usual one, I'm guessing you're eating for two, Sweetheart Mae. I figured it would only be a matter of time before our virile sheriff got you in the mama way. How's Decker takin' the news?"

Sweetie's smile was filled with love. "He's over the moon just like I am."

Mrs. Stokes nodded. "That's how it should be." Her gaze narrowed on Liberty. "If we're going by birth order, that means you're next."

Again there was the pang of pain, but Liberty ignored it. "No babies for me . . . or over-the-moon daddies."

"That's what we all think until we get bitten by the love bug." From what Liberty knew, Mrs. Stokes had been bitten quite a lot. "I figure you're about due."

Liberty might have argued some more if Mrs. Stokes hadn't had a coughing fit. Everyone knew you didn't talk during one of her fits. While Liberty was waiting for it to end, she heard a loud rumbling noise. The same loud rumbling noise she'd heard yesterday when she'd been helping her mama with the dinner dishes. She didn't even have to look down the street to know what was coming.

But she looked anyway.

The truck took up one and a half lanes. The way the shiny chrome grille was made it looked like the truck was grinning as it barreled toward them with flags flapping on either side like red, white, and blue flames.

"Good Lord," Cloe said. "What's that?"

"The annoying redneck I was telling you about," Liberty grumbled.

Sweetie sent her a warning look. "Remember how to catch flies, Libby."

Liberty hated that her sister was right. She might not like Jesse, but she needed to be nice to him. Just in case he did have the ability to sway Corbin.

She plastered on a smile as the truck pulled into two spaces. The door swung open and Jesse jumped out. He was wearing his standard outfit of white T-shirt, faded jeans, and the crumpled hat. It looked like he'd formed a truce with Taylor Swift because he was holding the kitten, its furry little head peeking out between his thumb and pointer finger. Even though Liberty didn't like the man, she had to admit the sight of the rough cowboy holding Tay-Tay caused a slight twinge in her heart.

He seemed to be lost in thought because he didn't notice Liberty until he was almost to the door of the café. He stopped in his tracks and those soft brown eyes locked on her. She tried to hold on to her smile, but it was hard when a wave of heat washed over her like she'd just stepped outside on a hot August day.

What the hell? Now all he had to do was look at her and she melted.

Thankfully, Sweetie hadn't lost her ability to speak. "You must be Jesse Cates." She held out a hand. "I'm Sweetie Carson."

Jesse pulled his gaze away from Liberty and shook Sweetie's hand. "Nice to meet you. I'd take off my hat, but my hands are kind of full."

"Aww, what a sweetheart." Sweetie went to pet Tay-Tay, but the kitten hissed and she pulled her hand back.

"Sorry," Jesse said. "She's meaner than a rattlesnake."

"Or maybe she just doesn't like strangers petting her." Cloe held out her hand. "Cloe Remington."

He took her hand. "Pleasure."

"So you're the one who adopted Taylor Swift," Mrs. Stokes said.

"Not me. I'm just cat-sitting for a friend. I didn't plan on bringing her this morning, but she's taken to slipping out the door whenever I open it."

"Cats do have minds of their own. I'm Fiona Stokes, by the way." Mrs. Stokes looked over at Liberty. "That's Liberty Holiday."

Jesse glanced at her. His normal cocky smile was missing. "Liberty and I have already met."

"Is that so?"

Liberty could hear the sly curiosity in Mrs. Stokes's voice and she tried to squelch it before the woman got the wrong idea. "We met yesterday at a business meeting."

Jesse's eyebrows lifted and for a second she

thought he was going to mention their first meeting at Cooper Springs. Instead, he nodded. "Purely business."

Mrs. Stokes looked between them. "I've had quite a few . . . business meetings myself over the years." She returned her attention to Jesse. "Cates. You wouldn't be related to the Cateses who own C-Corp, would you?"

Jesse hesitated before he answered. "As a matter of fact, I am."

"Then I guess you do know business. And speaking of business, I need to get to mine." She nodded at Sweetie and Cloe. "Congratulations, girls. It's about time we started repopulating this town." After adjusting her stole around her shoulders, she headed down the street.

When she was gone, Jesse looked at Cloe and Sweetie. "It was nice meeting y'all." He gave Liberty a brief nod before he turned to the door.

She stopped him. "Sheryl Ann doesn't allow animals in the café after Milford Riddle brought in his goat and she ate the chair cushions."

He didn't smile. Liberty was annoyed by how much she missed his cocky grin. "Then I guess I'll leave Tay-Tay in the truck." He started for his truck, but again she stopped him.

"I'll hold her for you."

He blinked, his eyes confused and distrusting. And she really couldn't blame him. She'd been all vinegar and now she was all sugar. He probably thought she had lost her mind. But talking with her sisters had made her reestablish her goal. If sucking up to a redneck kept her grandmother in her beloved home, she was willing to do some sucking. Which caused her to remember sucking his bottom lip into her mouth.

Her gaze lowered to his lips. By the time she realized what she was doing and glanced up, his eyes had darkened. The heated look made her tingle all over. She knew if they were alone, she'd be pressing herself against his hard body just like Tay-Tay was. He seemed to know it too because he looked away and cleared his throat.

"That's okay. Tay-Tay can stay in the truck. I won't be that long."

Maybe it was her need to succeed at her goal of saving the ranch. Or maybe it was her annoyance at being so easily brushed off. Whatever it was, Liberty couldn't let him refuse her offer.

"Don't be an irresponsible pet owner. It's too hot to leave her in the truck." She walked around the picnic table and took the kitten from him, ignoring the hard heat of his chest and the sharpness of Tay-Tay's teeth.

Jesse didn't say anything. All he did was give her one more confused look before he headed inside. When he was gone, Cloe patted her on the back.

"Now was that so hard?"

It was a lot harder than she'd thought. Mostly because she couldn't seem to control her body when he was around. "He's still one of the most annoying men I've ever met."

"You didn't seem that annoyed with him today." Sweetie smiled knowingly. "In fact, you looked like you were about to melt into the cement like a crayon left out in the sun too long."

Liberty scowled. "Very funny."

"Sweetie does have a point," Cloe said. "I think you're a little more taken with Jesse than you let us believe. And he must know something about business if Mrs. Stokes knows who his family is." She pulled out her cellphone and started tapping the screen. "C-Corp." Only a few seconds later, her eyes widened. "Oh my goodness."

"What?" Sweetie leaned over her shoulder and looked at her phone. Her eyes widened too. "Holy crap."

"Okay," Liberty said. "What's going on? Does C-Corp own carnivals? Because it would make sense." She glanced at the huge truck. "Jesse's a carnie if ever I saw one."

Cloe looked up from her phone and shook her head. "No, his family aren't carnies . . . they're billionaires."

Chapter Eight

JESSE DIDN'T KNOW what kind of spell Liberty Holiday had put on him, but he didn't like it. He didn't like that he'd been up half the night replaying their kisses. He didn't like that when he finally did fall asleep, he dreamed of doing a lot more to Liberty than kissing. And he didn't like that one look from those meadow-green eyes this morning and he'd had only one thought . . . *how can I get my lips back on hers?*

Even now, as he stood in line waiting to order his muffin and coffee, he couldn't help glancing out the window. All three of the Holiday sisters were beautiful in their own right, but Liberty stood out like a fiery ruby in a case of colorless diamonds.

She seemed to be embracing her country girl heritage. Today, she wore a T-shirt, blue jeans, and roper boots that looked well worn in. She wore a straw cowboy hat and had braided her hair into two cute braids that hung over the swells of her breasts. It was easy to picture her working the Holiday Ranch in that outfit—mucking out stalls and herding cattle. He bet she was a skilled cowgirl.

Liberty didn't do things half assed.

Last night when he couldn't keep the images of their kisses out of his head, he'd Googled her. It seemed Holiday Sisters Events was doing all right for themselves. He knew what went into a successful company and HSE had all the makings of a successful company. They had a great website, a healthy social media following ... and a determined and dedicated CEO Jesse couldn't help but admire. In almost every picture of every event, Liberty was pointing and issuing orders to caterers, florists, decorators, and her sister, who was always at her side.

Jesse knew they were twins. When he saw them in photographs together, he was still shocked by how much the two women looked alike. But no matter how identical they were, he had no problems telling them apart. Not only because Liberty was always dressed in power suits and heels while Belle dressed softer in more subdued feminine dresses and lower heels, but also because of the energy they exuded.

Belle seemed to be enjoying every event. Her body posture was relaxed, her eyes soft, and her smile warm as she adjusted veils and fluffed wedding gown trains and calmed nervous-looking grooms. Liberty didn't look like she was enjoying the events as much as beating them into submission. In every picture, she was always on the move, her eyes full of fire and her expression ferocious.

He knew that look. The need to succeed and

prove yourself. Corbin had it. And Jesse had had it too. But now that he had succeeded, he had to wonder what his success had proven. That he could make money? He could take care of himself and live his life without any help from anyone? Including his wealthy family?

His daddy, Billy, had wanted Jesse to be part of C-Corp, but Jesse had refused the offer. He had wanted to make it on his own. He had, but to what end?

His cellphone rang, pulling him out of his thoughts. He turned away from the window and took his phone out of his pocket. It was Corbin and he quickly answered it.

"Hey, Whitty. Where have you been, man? I've been trying to get ahold of you."

"I didn't pack the right power adapter and I couldn't charge my phone until today. So I just got your message . . . and Liberty Holiday's. What was she doing using your phone?"

"She was the one who called the meeting. Not Hank."

He thought Corbin would be surprised. He wasn't. "I thought as much. So I guess she's pissed."

"I'd say more confused. As am I, after hearing about Rome Remington's offer to pay off the loan." He started to ask for more details when he realized that the people around him had stopped their conversations and were listening in. The woman sitting at a nearby table in the brightly colored shirt and Crocs was leaning so far out of her chair he was surprised she wasn't on the floor. Having grown up in a small town, he had no doubt that whatever he talked about with Corbin would be all over town by this afternoon. He returned to his phone conversation. "Look, I can't really talk right now. I'll call you back in a few minutes."

"That won't work for me. I'm walking into a restaurant to meet Sunny."

Jesse wished he could step outside and continue the call, but then he'd be right in the middle of the Holiday sisters. Which would be even worse. "Okay, then call me when you get done."

"Will do."

When Jesse stepped up to the counter, he had so much trouble deciding which muffin looked the best that he ended up ordering a half dozen. Which made Sheryl Ann beam with happiness as she started filling his order.

"I'm glad you enjoyed the Cocoa Java Junkie so much that you came back. I'm Sheryl Ann, by the way. I didn't catch your name the last time you were in."

"Nice to meet you, Sheryl Ann. I'm Jesse Cates. And I couldn't stay away after the best muffin I've ever had."

Her smile got even bigger. "So where are you staying, Jesse?"

"I'm staying at a friend's place for a few days and cat-sitting while he's gone."

The woman in the brightly colored Crocs spoke. "Corbin Whitlock?"

Damn. He'd hoped to remain incognito. But it looked like that wasn't going to happen. He pinned on a smile. "Yes, ma'am. Do you know him?"

She and Sheryl Ann exchanged looks. They weren't good looks. The woman in the Crocs stood and Jesse braced for a cussing out. "I'm Melba Wadley, the one who gave Corbin Taylor Swift."

Gave was a bad choice of words. *Forced* seemed more accurate. Corbin had told Jesse the story about how Melba wouldn't take no for an answer.

"We all know Corbin," Sheryl Ann cut in. "He used to live here. He seemed like a nice boy back then. Mannerly, hardworking, and honest." She rang up his order on the old cash register. "But I changed my opinion after hearing about him foreclosing on the Holidays' beloved ranch. We now refer to him as Corbin Whiplash."

Jesse couldn't help but laugh. As a kid, he'd loved the *Dudley Do-Right* movie with the villain Snidely Whiplash.

Melba shot him a narrow-eyed look. "It's not funny. If I had known Corbin had become a cold-hearted loan shark, I never would have given him sweet Taylor Swift."

Sweet? Obviously, the woman didn't know the kitten well.

Jesse glanced around at all the people scowling at him. He knew enough about loyal small-town folks to know he was seconds away from being tarred and feathered.

He sobered. "There's no need to worry about Taylor Swift, ma'am. Corbin loves the kitten as much as he loves his sister—and that's a helluva lot. Pardon my language."

"Now that you mention it," Melba said. "I remember how sweet he was to his little sister. He rode her around all over town on the handlebars of that bike Mrs. Stokes gave him."

"I remember that too," Sheryl Ann joined in. "I guess a man can't be all bad if he loves his sister and kittens." She looked at Jesse. "But kicking a family out of their home is just plain wrong."

Jesse didn't disagree. But until he talked with Corbin, he wasn't about to agree either. "I'm sure it will all get figured out once Corbin gets back into town." He quickly paid. "Thanks for the best muffins in Texas, Sheryl Ann." He tucked the box of muffins under his arm and picked up his to-go cup of coffee before he turned to leave.

Melba blocked his way.

"You got a pet?"

"No, ma'am. I travel too much for a pet."

She scowled. "That's no reason not to have a fur baby. Small dogs and cats can travel on planes as long as you have an approved pet carrier. Buck Owens is a little overweight, but he's still under the twenty-pound limit and I know he'd be the perfect traveling companion. If you come on over to the sheriff's office, I'll introduce you."

"I sure do appreciate the offer, but I'm afraid I have to pass." He scrambled for an excuse. "I have a . . . date with Liberty Holiday." It wasn't a lie. He did have to get Tay-Tay back from her.

Melba's eyebrows shot up. Everyone else in the café looked surprised too. Jesse took their stunned silence as an opportunity to make his escape. Coach Denny stopped him at the door and spoke in a low voice.

"You better buy yourself a sturdy cup, boy, because that little gal is a ballbuster if ever there was one."

Once outside, Jesse heaved a sigh of relief and looked around for the Holiday sisters. They were gone. And so was Tay-Tay. Damn it! He'd known Liberty's sweetness was all an act. She'd catnapped his kitten.

He headed for his truck with the intention of searching up and down the street, but stopped short when he saw Liberty sitting in the passenger seat. There was something about her in his beloved truck that made him feel a little lightheaded. It took a firm mental shake and a long gulp of black coffee to get his head feeling normal and his feet moving again.

"What are you doing?" he asked as he opened the driver's door. The rest of what he was going to say got lost somewhere in his brain when he saw that she was sitting cross-legged on the seat with Tay-Tay sleeping in the nest she'd made of those long, tanned legs. He wanted to take the kitten's place so badly his hands shook.

Completely unaware of his battle with his libido, Liberty stroked the kitten's head. "Tay-Tay was not happy being held. I have the scratch marks to prove it. And since I didn't want to put her down and risk her running into the street and becoming roadkill, I decided we'd wait for you in here."

"I thought a pet in a hot vehicle was a bad thing."

"Well, it's certainly not a good thing." She changed *thing* into a sexy Texas *thang* that made his belly feel all airy as she fanned a hand in front of her face. "So don't just stand there. Get in and start up this beast. I'm assuming it has air-conditioning. Or is this redneck monstrosity wind cooled only?"

Even though the last *thang* he wanted was to be enclosed in a small space with Liberty, he set the box of muffins on the seat and climbed in. Once the engine was rumbling and the air-conditioning flowing from the vents, he turned to her.

"What's going on?"

She lifted a dark eyebrow. "I just told you. Tay was scratching the heck out of me to get down."

"I'm not talking about that. I'm talking about you volunteering to watch Taylor in the first place and no longer treating me like cow dung stuck to the heel of your boot. Last night, you couldn't get rid of me fast enough and today you're acting like we're friends."

She shrugged. "Maybe I've had a change of heart."

"Oh, really. And what brought about this change of heart?"

She hesitated for only a second before she answered him. "I realized that you might be the only one who can change Corbin's mind about foreclosing on Holiday Ranch. That's if you really are friends with him."

Now would be a good time to tell her the truth

about his relationship with Corbin and that he owned a portion of Oleander Investments. But he knew if he came clean now, Liberty would assume the worst and think he was in cahoots with Corbin. He shouldn't care about what Liberty thought. She was nothing to him. But for some reason, he did care.

He cared a lot.

"So that's why you've decided to suck up to me," he said. "You need my help."

"Why else would I be willing to cat-sit this ornery animal?" She stroked the kitten's tiny ear and Tay-Tay growled low, causing Liberty to laugh.

The transformation that took place when Liberty laughed made heat flood his body. Which was ridiculous. She'd flat-out told him the only reason she was being nice was to get him to change Corbin's mind, but for some reason Jesse's mind had latched on to the idea of Liberty sucking up and wouldn't let it go.

Getting involved with her was a bad idea. A very bad idea. His gut knew this. But the desire pooling inside him like the steaming hot coffee he still held in his hand overrode his gut.

In business, he had always liked to have the upper hand. To have something someone wanted badly was called bargaining power. With it, Jesse had always gotten what he wanted. Even if it wasn't a good idea, he wanted Liberty. He wanted her with an intensity that scared the shit out of him.

If she hadn't turned the tables on him and

started being nice, he might have been able to avoid her. But when she was sitting right next to him, offering him the power to have her, he couldn't refuse it.

He wasn't a stupid man.

"What else?" he asked.

She blinked. "What do you mean?"

"What else would you be willing to do to get me to change Corbin's mind? Ass kissing usually entails doing more than one thing for the—"

She cut in. "Ass you're kissing?"

He laughed because he couldn't help it. He didn't just desire her. He liked her. "As a matter of fact, yes. So what else are you going to do for this ass, Libby Lou?"

The annoyed look in her eyes said she was only seconds away from telling him to go to hell. But instead, she took a deep breath and slowly released it as the logical businesswoman took over.

"I won't just cat-sit for a few minutes. I'll take Tay-Tay to the ranch and cat-sit until Corbin gets back. Mimi has missed having animals around and will love it."

"Hmm?" He took a sip of coffee. "It would certainly be nice to not have to worry every night about my throat being ripped open by kitty claws. But a little cat-sitting in exchange for what you're asking doesn't seem like quite enough."

He was toying with her . . . and loving every second of it.

Anger flashed in her emerald eyes, but she didn't concede. He knew she wouldn't.

"Fine. I'm one of the best event planners in

Texas . . . if not the best. If you can talk Corbin into stopping the foreclosure proceedings and letting Rome pay off the loan, I'll do an event for you for free. I'm talking everything from the tables to the decorations to the invitations to the dessert forks. Everything."

"I'm not really a guy who likes to host big events. What else?"

She gritted her teeth. "You seemed to love pigging out on my mama's apple pie. She'll make you as many as you want until you leave. And dinner. Dinner every night."

"That's a nice offer, but that's your mama sucking up. Not you. I want to know what you're willing to give for your family to keep their ranch."

Her fists tightened and he braced for a punch. "Fine," she said through her teeth. "I'll make you dinner and apple pie."

His eyes widened. "You know how to cook?"

"Why do you find that so surprising?"

"Because you're not really the homemaker type."

"And exactly what is the homemaker type? Just because I run my own business doesn't mean I don't enjoy cooking, baking, and sewing."

"Sewing? Now you are joking."

She glared at him. "You are the most insufferable man I have ever met in my life. Yes, I can sew. I'd love to sew a zipper over your arrogant mouth right now."

He grinned. "I'd just unzip it. I'm a whiz with zippers."

Her eyes narrowed. "So that's it, isn't it? You don't want apple pie from me. Or event planning. Or cat-sitting. You want to force me into giving you sexual favors." The thought of Liberty giving him sexual favors had all the blood in his body heading south. But, on the other hand, the *force* part pissed him off.

"I have never forced a woman into giving me sexual favors in my life and I never will. What a woman does for me in bed, she does of her own free will. I would never push a woman to do something she didn't want to do."

She snorted. "You just push them into bets to get what you want."

"Now, darlin', you didn't have to take that bet . . . or cheat."

"I did not cheat! And even if I did, you ended up getting your kiss and an extra one to boot."

"So you're now saying that the only reason you kissed me was because of our bet. And here I thought it was boredom."

She crossed her arms. "The second kiss was boredom. The first was because I always pay my debts in full. Something you need to point out to your friend, but not if it means I have to hop into bed with the likes of you."

It was amazing how much this woman could piss him off.

"I wasn't the one who brought up sexual favors," he said. "I believe that was you. Which leads me to believe you're the one who wants to swap sex for the deed to the ranch."

"As if! A ranch isn't worth having sex with an arrogant rodeo bum."

He lifted an eyebrow. "Those two kisses we shared said just the opposite, darlin'. I bet if we spent any time together, you'd be the one begging me for sexual favors."

Her eyes widened. "Like hell I would!"

"You want to bet on it?"

Her eyes flashed fire. "You bet I want to bet on it!"

"Great. If you can keep yourself from falling into bed with this arrogant rodeo bum by the time Corbin gets back into town, I'll talk him into letting Rome pay off the loan."

She opened her mouth, but he held up a finger.

"But you have to spend time with me."

"How much time?"

"As much as I want."

She studied him for a long moment and he could almost see the wheels of her mind working. The wheels of his mind were working too. What in the hell was he doing? He had decided starting something up with Liberty was a bad idea and now here he was starting something up with her. All because he wanted to prove a point.

Of course, that wasn't all it was.

He wanted Liberty. He wanted her like he'd never wanted another woman. So why couldn't he have her? Not forever. Just for a while. It wasn't like she was a woman hunting for a man to spend the rest of her life with. Like him, she was too wrapped up in making money to want a serious relationship. Which made it a perfect arrangement.

Of course, if she won, he'd have to talk Corbin into letting Rome pay off the loan. Jesse never went back on a bet. And maybe that wouldn't be such a bad idea. Letting Rome pay off the ranch was a smart business move. Not just financially, but also for public relations. For whatever reason, Corbin had an attachment to this town. Otherwise, he wouldn't still be hanging on to the beat-up trailer his uncle had willed him. If he foreclosed on the Holiday Ranch, the townsfolk were likely to run him out of town on a rail.

That wouldn't be good for anyone.

Of course, Jesse wasn't about to tell Liberty about his change of heart and give up this game.

A game he planned to win.

"So?" he said with a slight smirk he knew would goad her. "Is the bet on? Or are you too afraid of losing?"

Chapter Nine

Liberty should tell Jesse to take a flying leap at a rolling donut. Being at the arrogant cowboy's beck and call was the worst thing she could possibly imagine. Not only because he annoyed the hell out of her, but also because there were times that he didn't. Times when she caught herself actually enjoying their sparring. As much as she hated to admit it, he had a quick wit and an easy charm that entertained her. She couldn't remember the last time a man had entertained her.

Or caused her panties to feel like they'd been set aflame with just one look.

Which is why she should probably decline the bet. After two heated kisses, she had come to realize she was more than a little sexually attracted to Jesse Cates. And today had only solidified that realization.

Being this close to him had her libido doing jumping jacks. Every time he took a sip of coffee, she couldn't help watching the way his bottom lip curved under the rim of the take-out cup. The way he sipped the hot liquid into his mouth. The way he licked away any wayward drops. All she wanted to do was jerk him to her and suck the steamy caffeinated flavor from his mouth.

If she couldn't sit in a truck with him and not want to devour him, the chances of her winning the bet were slim to none.

But she had no choice. She had to take the bet.

After discovering Jesse was related to one of the most influential families in Texas, she realized he had more clout than she'd thought. He wasn't just Corbin's friend. He was a powerful friend. If Corbin was any kind of a smart businessman, he'd take whatever advice Jesse gave him. In business, keeping powerful people as friends was important.

Which was another reason Liberty was considering the bet.

The Cates were one of the wealthiest families in Texas. And wealthy families always needed a good event planner. If she could resist falling in bed with Jesse and instead just become his friend, she could not only save her family's ranch, but she could also get new clients for Holiday Sisters Events. Clients who would recommend her and Belle to all their influential friends.

All she had to do was stay strong.

If Liberty was anything, she was strong.

She held out her hand. "Deal."

Jesse hesitated for only a second before he took it. She had shaken a lot of men's hands in her life. Arrogant men who held her hand too softly because they thought of her as a weak woman and insecure men who squeezed too hard to prove their strength and power. Jesse's handshake was neither. His calloused fingers gripped hers with just enough pressure to make her feel respected, but not enough to make her feel threatened.

"Deal." He grinned. "Now you're not planning on running off like you did at Cooper Springs, are you?"

"I believe I swam off. And you just weren't fast enough to catch me. Maybe you need to brush up on your chasing skills."

His smile faded as his brown eyes turned steamy. "Maybe I do. How about I start by taking you to dinner tonight?"

The last thing she should do if she wanted to win the bet was to go on a date alone with him. She needed to make sure they were never alone.

"Sorry, but I already told my mama I'd cook dinner tonight. You're welcome to come. In fact, let me give you my number." She took a pen out of her purse and wrote the number on the lid of the muffin box, finishing by scrawling her name at the top.

He looked at the name she'd written. "I thought you didn't like me calling you Libby Lou."

"I figure the more it annoys me, the more you'll use it. So I'm embracing it. You'll have to come up with something else to annoy me."

"I'm sure that won't be hard."

She laughed. "I'm sure it won't be either."

A smile spread over his face. Not a cocky one. A sincere one. Like he was looking forward to seeing just how much he could annoy her. She had to admit she was looking forward to it too. She hadn't lied when she'd told him she was bored. But now, suddenly, she wasn't bored at all. She had a challenge. She loved a good challenge.

She looked down at Tay-Tay sleeping in her lap. "You want to get your cat? I'd like to save some of my skin."

"Sorry, but we made a deal. You're taking Tay-Tay home."

She stared at him. "That was before our bet."

"Right. But you still offered and I'm accepting. I'll bring all her designer cat things when I come for dinner tonight."

"Talk about a cheater," she grumbled as she tucked the kitten against her chest. She only cringed slightly when Tay-Tay dug her claws into her hand. "But good luck getting me into your bed with my daddy and his shotgun standing guard."

He shrugged. "I've outsmarted many a shotgun-toting daddy."

"But you won't outsmart me." She opened the door. But before she jumped down from the big truck, she flipped up the lid of the box and grabbed a muffin.

"Hey!" he said. "That's my Cocoa Java Junkie."

"Consider it part of your seduction. I love dark chocolate and coffee. I also love diamond earrings—at least one carat, Ferragamo shoes—red, and Gucci handbags—any." She sent him a cocky grin. "Sorry, but you didn't choose a cheap gal to seduce." She took a big bite of the muffin as she nudged the door closed with her shoulder.

She could hear his laughter all the way to her

car. Once she was behind the wheel of the SUV with Tay-Tay sitting in the passenger's seat, her cellphone pinged with an incoming text. She set the muffin in the cup holder and reached in her purse for her phone. She didn't recognize the number, but she knew who the text was from as soon as she read it.

What size shoe?

She smiled as she texted back. Nine and a half.

He replied almost immediately. Those are some good-sized hoofs, Libby Lou. I know what they say about men who have big feet. What do they say about women?

She rolled her eyes. Are you asking if I have a big penis?

Well, considering everyone in town has told me you have balls . . .

She laughed. Is this what you call seduction?

Is it working?

Not at all.

Then I guess it's back to the drawing board.

She was still smiling when a loud rumbling drew her attention. She glanced in her side mirror and saw his truck backing out behind her. He leaned down and waggled his fingers.

Annoying man.

She was watching the obnoxious truck take off with flags flapping when Melba Wadley startled her by stepping up to her window.

Melba had been the sheriff's assistant for as long as Liberty could remember. She was a stout woman with an addiction to Crocs, bright clothing, and abandoned or abused animals. She fostered those animals and found them permanent homes. Decker and Sweetie had two of Melba's orphans. Rome and Cloe had numerous. Corbin had one.

Which was why Liberty wasn't surprised when she rolled down the window to say hi and Tay-Tay jumped up and started meowing like crazy.

"Well, hey there, Taylor Swift." Melba stroked the kitten's ears—without one nip or scratch. "You're lookin' good, girlfriend. Love the rhinestone collar. I started getting a little concerned I'd made the wrong decision placing you with Corbin after I found out about what he's doing. But you look as fit as a fiddle." She glanced at Liberty. "How did you end up with her?"

"I'm just cat-sitting for a friend."

Melba looked surprised. "Jesse said y'all were friends, but I didn't believe him. Not when his friend is trying to take your family's ranch."

"It's complicated." That was putting it mildly, but Liberty didn't want the entire town finding out about her bet with Jesse. She didn't even want her family knowing. Her daddy would throw a fit. Her mama would be appalled that she'd even considered it, her sisters would try to talk her out of it, and Mimi . . . Mimi would probably think she was going to marry off another granddaughter. Which was why it was better to keep the bet to herself.

Of course, the townsfolk had always filled in the blanks the way they saw fit. Liberty was surprised how close Melba came to the truth.

"Ahh, I get it." She winked at Liberty. "That

Jesse is one hot cowboy. He turned his charming smile on me and I about melted into a puddle. And just because he's friends with Corbin doesn't mean he's a bad apple too. Although he refused to take Buck Owens." Melba's eyes lit up. "Say, you wouldn't be interested in a cute little pug, would you? Buck would be a perfect pet for you and Belle. I bet you two girls miss being around animals."

It was the truth. Liberty did miss animals. It hadn't been so bad when she and Belle could come back to the ranch and get their fix. But Daddy had to sell off all the cattle and horses to pay the loan. As the dogs and cats passed, Mama figured it was best not to replace them since she already had her hands full taking care of the ranch. It was a shame. Mimi and Mama loved cats and dogs.

As soon as Liberty untangled this mess, she intended to make sure they got as many as they wanted. Maybe she'd even buy Daddy a couple horses. He wouldn't have enough land to raise cattle, but he could ride. And she was sure Rome would let his new father-in-law help work the Remington Ranch. Although she doubted her daddy would want to. He and Sam Remington, Rome's father, put up with each other now that their children were married, but that didn't mean they liked each other.

". . . I'm telling you that Buck Owens is the sweetest thing you'd ever want to meet. Wait right here and I'll go get him."

Liberty pulled out of her thoughts and realized

she hadn't been paying close enough attention to what Melba was saying. If you didn't pay attention to Melba, you ended up with a pet you didn't want.

Liberty held up her hand. "Now hold up there, Mel. I'm sorry, but Belle and I can't take any of your animals. Our apartment building doesn't allow pets."

Melba looked like Liberty had punched her in the face. "What kind of place doesn't allow pets? And why would you and Belle want to live there?"

"Apartments close to our office are hard to find. Especially in our price range."

Melba sighed. "I guess I just don't understand city life. But Buck Owens isn't why I wanted to talk to you, anyway. My granddaughter is going to turn five this Saturday and since my daughter-in-law has her hands full with my three-year-old granddaughter and my new grandson, I told her I'd pull Pip's party together. But I don't know the first thing about planning a little girl's party and I was wondering if you'd help me out."

When Liberty had started an event-planning business with Belle, no kids' parties had been her one stipulation.

"Sorry, Mel, but kids' birthday parties aren't really my specialty. Belle and I only do adult events."

"I just need a little guidance. My sons you could hand squirt guns and Popsicles and they thought it was a party. But little girls are different. They like everything organized and pretty with planned entertainment. I don't have a clue how to entertain twelve little girls."

"Then why did you volunteer?"

A sad look entered Melba's eyes. "I guess I was just hoping to score some points with my granddaughter. Her other grandma is real creative—always making her cute little tutus and coming up with fun games and craft ideas for them to do together. When I invite Pip over, all she gets to do is help me take care of my foster animals."

"Which I'm sure she loves."

Melba smiled. "She does. She's a chip off the old block. She says she's going to be a veterinarian when she grows up. I don't doubt it with the way she helps me out." Her eyes turned hopeful. "Which is why I'd like to do something really special for her. I could pay you."

Liberty knew Melba couldn't afford to pay Holiday Sisters Events prices. Not that Liberty would ever take money from her . . . nor could she deny the woman help. No matter how much it hurt to be around little kids. And since her sisters were pregnant, she needed to quit being a wussy and get over her phobia.

"I'll help you," she said. "But not for money. After everything you've done for my family and this town, I'll be happy to do a party for your granddaughter free of charge."

Melba's eyes widened. "Oh, I couldn't let you do that. I'd have to give you something. You sure you don't want Buck Owens?"

"I'm sure." Liberty lifted her phone and opened

her notes. "Now what else does your granddaughter like besides animals?"

Once she'd gotten all the information she needed from Melba, Liberty headed back to the ranch. On the way, Belle called. This was the longest they had been apart. Just hearing her voice made Liberty feel happy.

"Belly!"

"Libby!"

"I miss you," they said at the same time, and then laughed.

"So how are things going?" Liberty asked.

Belle quickly filled Liberty in on everything that had been happening since the last time they spoke—all the events she'd just hosted and all the ones coming up on the calendar. Belle had an entire list of things she wanted Liberty to help her decide on. Decision-making was not Belle's forte. She worried too much about making mistakes. Liberty, on the other hand, didn't worry at all about making the wrong decision.

Her bet with Jesse being a perfect example.

"Go with the low arrangements of hydrangeas instead of the high tulips," she said. "That way people can talk to the people seated across the table from them."

"As always, you're right, Libby," Belle said. "Hydrangeas it is. Oh, and the rental price of tables and chairs has gone up again. Maybe we should think about buying our own. It would be expensive at first, but save us money in the long run."

"I agree that it would save money, but where

would we store them? Our office space is jam-packed as is with decorations and event supplies."

"Our lease is coming up. Maybe we should start looking for a new space. One with a larger storage area."

"That will cost money too."

"You're right. But it never hurts to look. Maybe we'll stumble on a real bargain."

"I won't be stumbling on anything, there's still no Wi-Fi at the ranch. I swear it's like living in a dead zone."

Belle laughed. "It's always been that way. If it's making you go crazy, I'll be happy to come early and help sort things out there while you take over here."

Liberty would love to take her up on the offer, but it wouldn't be fair. All the sisters were taking a turn helping out at the ranch. Liberty couldn't shirk her responsibility.

That, and there was the bet to consider.

"No, it's fine. I need to stay here because there have been some new developments. Corbin knows it's our ranch he's foreclosing on."

There was a long stretch of silence before Belle spoke. "So I guess the meeting with him didn't go well."

"He didn't show up. He's in Paris with his sister. He sent his friend." She quickly filled her sister in on all the details. Then because she had never kept anything from her twin sister, she told her about the two kisses and the bet. Belle did not sound happy about any of it.

"Oh, Lib, this isn't good."

"It will be if I win."

"But what if you don't? If you've already kissed Jesse twice, you must be physically attracted to him."

Liberty couldn't deny it. "That doesn't mean I'm going to fall into bed with him. Especially now that keeping the family home depends upon it. You know me, Belly. When it comes to a challenge, I never lose. I'm going to win the bet, get the ranch back . . . and keep the barn that's going to be a perfect wedding venue for our business. Now enough about Jesse. Have you talked to Sweetie? It looks like we're going to need to plan two baby showers instead of just one."

"Sweetie's pregnant! Oh my gosh! That's wonderful news." Belle hesitated. "How do you feel about it?"

She had never been able to lie to her twin. "A little jealous, but it will pass."

"You could still be a mom, Libby. That doctor didn't say you couldn't get pregnant. He just said it was highly unlikely."

"I think he was just trying to leave me with a little hope. But I've seen pictures of my scans and ultrasounds, Belly. I have so much scar tissue on my ovaries from endometrial cysts, they look like peach pits. Besides, getting married and having a passel of snot-nosed kids has never been my dream. I'll be just fine being awesome Auntie Libby."

And maybe if she kept telling herself that, she would be.

Chapter Ten

Jesse should have known Liberty would play the game well. As soon as he arrived at the Holiday Ranch, she pawned him off on Mimi.

"Why don't you take Jesse to see your gardens, Mimi? I'm sure he would love to see all the vegetables and flowers you grow." Liberty flashed him a smug smile. "Wouldn't you, Jesse? Mimi is one of the best gardeners in all of Texas."

It turned out Liberty wasn't wrong. Mimi knew how to garden. She pointed out every flower in the front garden and told him their names and what they needed to bloom so brilliantly before she took him around back and showed off her extensive vegetable garden.

While she gave him a tour, she talked about how long the land had been in the Holiday family. He knew she was making her case so he'd talk Corbin into stopping the foreclosure proceedings.

He had tried, but he and Corbin were playing telephone tag. It was easy to do when there was a seven-hour time difference and Corbin was busy spoiling his little sister. But Jesse wasn't worried.

No matter what his reason was for wanting the ranch, Jesse knew Corbin was a deep-down good man. He wouldn't take the Holidays' home away from them. There had to be a misunderstanding. One Jesse would get figured out once Corbin got back.

"Liberty mentioned you're adopted."

Mimi's comment pulled him from his thoughts and he returned his attention to the older woman. She wore her wide-brimmed hat, T-shirt, and jeans again. Tay-Tay was cradled in her arms. That cat loved the old woman and the feeling seemed to be mutual.

"Yes, ma'am," he said. "I was adopted when I was nine and happily so."

She petted Tay-Tay. "And before that, you were in foster care?"

"I don't know if I'd call it care."

Mimi smiled. "I knew we had a strong bond the first time we met. I lost both my parents when I was fourteen and ended up in foster care. The family I lived with was good to me, but they didn't want to adopt a sullen teenager. I can't say as I blame them. I was filled with a lot of hate back then."

Jesse understood perfectly. "I was pretty angry myself."

She nodded. "I think anger is what kids go to when they don't understand why bad things happen. But it looks like we found our happiness. You got good adoptive parents and I met the love of my life and he gave me this." She looked around and smiled.

That pretty much clinched it. There was no way he could let Corbin foreclose on the ranch now.

When they got to the house, Hank and Darla were sitting on the porch swing enjoying the last rays of the sun. He could tell Hank still wasn't thrilled he was there, but he wasn't quite as mean looking as he'd been on Jesse's first visit. Darla was gracious as always.

"Come join us, Jesse. It's a lovely sunset."

"It sure is, ma'am. Where's Liberty?"

"She wanted to make supper by herself and shooed me out of the kitchen." Darla's eyes twinkled. "I think she wants to impress you."

Or more like hide from him.

He smiled. "Well, I can't let her go to all the trouble without a little help."

When he walked into the kitchen, he found Liberty elbow deep in chopped vegetables. She was wearing an old-fashioned gingham apron that looked like it had been passed down from generation to generation. Why the sight of her in it made his heart trip was beyond him.

He had come in to start his seduction, but he discovered he was content to just stand in the doorway and watch her chop an onion. He didn't realize it had made her cry until she glanced up. Seeing tears glistening in those emerald eyes totally wrecked him. Thankfully, her sassy smile kept him from rushing over and pulling her into his arms to soothe her.

"Did you have fun with Mimi?"

He moved to the island she stood at. "As a matter of fact, I did. You were right. She's quite the master gardener. Did you know she already has tomatoes on the vine?" He pulled a paper towel off the roll sitting on the counter, then took her chin in his hand. The feel of the baby-soft skin under that stubborn chin had him feeling light-headed with the need to place his lips there. But he pushed down the desire and concentrated on gently wiping the tears from her cheeks.

Cheeks that now held a deep flush.

It seemed Liberty wasn't immune to his touch either. He ran his thumb over her plump bottom lip and kept his voice low since the window was open that led to the porch. "I love sweet . . . ripe . . . tomatoes right off the vine." He watched heat fill her eyes. But a split second later, it was replaced by a determined look and she pulled away.

"I bet you do. I'm sure you've had your fair share of sweet ripe tomatoes straight off the vine. Now as you can see, I'm pretty busy. So why don't you head on into the living room and watch *Wheel of Fortune* until supper's ready? I know how much you enjoy playing games."

He did love a good game. But the best one was going on right here with Liberty. He rolled up the sleeves of his western shirt.

"Thanks, Libby Lou, but I happen to love helping out in the kitchen. In fact, why don't you let me take over chopping those veggies? I'd hate for you to get more tears in your eyes and cut off one of those pretty little fingers." He started to reach for the knife, but stopped short when she pointed it at him.

"No need. I'm an expert with a knife. But if you insist on helping me . . ." She used the knife to point at an apron hanging on a hook. "Why don't you put that apron on, wash your hands, and start rolling some buns."

His gaze lowered to the sweet curves of her butt in the tight jeans peeking out from the bowstrings of the apron. "Now you're talking my language. Buns are my specialty."

"Again, I'm not surprised."

He laughed as he slipped on the apron and tied it. She laughed when he was finished.

"My, my, don't you look pretty in blue ruffles."

"You should see me in pink. It really brings out the red of my hair." He rubbed his hands together. "Where are the buns? I'm ready to get at them." Again, he eyed her butt. She just rolled her eyes and pointed the knife at a bowl with a dish towel over it.

"Have at it."

Since he'd had to fend for himself at an early age, Jesse knew his way around a kitchen. But his cooking skills only went as far as easily prepared foods like box macaroni and cheese, frozen pizzas, and canned chili. Dinner rolls were beyond his culinary expertise. But he wasn't about to let Liberty know that. Especially when she was watching him with a smug smile.

After washing his hands, he headed over to the dish towel-covered bowl and got to work. He knew what rolls should look like. He just didn't know how to get them from the big ball of dough to the golden-brown fluffiness he loved. He figured you just grabbed a glob of dough and rolled it. How hard could that be?

It turned out to be harder than he thought. It wasn't the rolling-them-into-balls part that was hard. It was more the getting-them-all-the-same-size part. Either he pinched off a piece of dough too big or pinched off one too little. By the time he'd finished filling the greased cookie sheet Liberty had given him, not any two rolls were the same size ... or the same shape.

Something Liberty found quite amusing.

"If that's what you think balls look like, I'm a little worried."

"No need to worry. My balls are just fine." He looked down at his misshapen rolls and scowled. They were pretty bad.

"Now there's no need to look so depressed, darlin'." She patted him on the butt on her way past. "We can't all be good at handling buns."

Despite his difficulty making dinner rolls, Jesse was enjoying himself. It wasn't the cooking he was enjoying as much as watching Liberty. She had been right. She could cook. She had the chicken and vegetables in the oven in the time it took him to do half a tray of rolls.

But it wasn't her expertise he enjoyed watching as much as her. Gone was the intense, bossy woman he'd seen in the pictures on the Holiday Sisters Events website and in her place was a much more relaxed, smiling woman.

Once the rolls were covered for the second rise, he leaned on the counter and watched as she added something to the cherry mixture she was making on the stove.

"Do you cook a lot in Houston?" he asked.

"Not as much as I'd like. I'm usually working until late at night so I grab something at whatever event I'm at or just have popcorn or a bowl of cereal when I get home."

He hadn't given much thought to the hours an event planner worked until now. Most events he'd attended were at night or on the weekends. "I guess your business doesn't leave much free time?

She snorted as she made a salad. "Much? Try none. Belle and I work until late every night and all weekend. But that's what happens when you run your own business. It's up to you to make it a success."

"Why event planning? You could run a business that has better hours." From what he'd seen, she would be kick ass at running any business.

"Event planning was Belle's dream." She smiled. Not the smile she usually gave him. This smile was soft and filled with love . . . and caused an ache deep down inside him that he couldn't explain. "My sister has always loved a good celebration. Holidays, birthdays, weddings, anniversaries. You should see her face when a bride walks down the aisle. Or a golden wedding anniversary couple redo their wedding vows. Or a ninety-year-old man blows out his birthday candles. She just loves to see people happy."

"And you don't?"

"It's not that. It's just I'm more a realist. I know

the bride walking down the aisle has a forty-percent chance of getting divorced. The golden anniversary couple has probably gone through hell and back to get to fifty years. And the ninety-year-old man would probably rather be back at his care facility watching *The Price Is Right* than there with his family who doesn't even come to visit him more than once a month."

"Obviously, you're the type of person who looks on the bright side," he said.

She laughed. "I guess I'm not a realist as much as a pessimist."

"So it's not your dream you're working the long hours for, it's your sister's?"

She shrugged. "I don't really have a dream. So why wouldn't I help Belle achieve hers?"

"You don't have a dream? I don't believe that. Everyone has a dream. Even if it's a small one."

A look passed over her face. A look of . . . longing? But it was gone before Jesse could be sure.

"Not me," she said. "Dreams rely on too many variables. I like goals much better. When I set goals, I know exactly what I have to do to achieve them. I make a list of smaller goals to meet the bigger one."

"And what smaller goals have you made to win the bet with me? Besides avoidance."

She smiled evilly. "As if I'm going to tell you. Never share your secrets with your opponent."

He tipped his head. "Are we opponents? Because it's starting to feel like we're friends."

"Do you always seduce your friends?"

"I don't have a lot of friends—males or females. I move around too much."

"What about Corbin? I thought he was your friend."

He realized he'd stepped right into that one. For a moment, he thought about telling her that Corbin was his half brother. But then he thought better of it. It would only make her distrust him more. For some reason, and not just winning the bet, he wanted her trust.

"He is, but he's about it."

She nodded. "I don't have a lot of friends either. But my reason has more to do with being too busy."

He hesitated. "Then maybe we should give friendship a try." Where had that come from? Liberty looked as surprised as he felt.

Her eyes widened. "Are you saying you no longer plan to seduce me?"

"Oh, no, I plan to seduce you. A bet is a bet. But I don't know why we can't be friends too." He uncrossed his arms and straightened. "Now what can I screw up next, Madam Chef?"

Surprisingly, the dinner rolls didn't turn out half bad once they were baked. They looked like some kind of blistered skin disease, but they tasted good. The rest of the meal was amazing. Jesse ate seconds of the roasted chicken and thirds of the roasted parsnips. He'd never had roasted parsnips, but he would from now on.

When dinner was over, he volunteered to clean up. At least that was something he was proficient at. Shirlene and Billy hadn't made their kids cook, but they were firm believers in everyone helping to clean up. Mimi and Darla started to help, but he shooed them out of the kitchen. Liberty didn't offer. As soon as he started clearing the table, she headed out the back door. He figured she wouldn't make it easy for him to find her before he had to leave.

"You better watch yourself, boy."

He turned to see Hank standing there giving him the evil eye. "Excuse me, sir?"

"My wife and mama seem to think you're a good man who will turn out to be our savior. I think you're a slick-talkin' con artist who has set his sights on my daughter and is willing to play both sides of the fence to get what he wants." Hank pointed a finger at him. "But I'll tell you this. Taking the ranch is one thing—I can't hold you or Corbin accountable when I'm the one responsible for getting my mama to sign that contract—but my baby girl is another matter. You hurt her and I promise I'll do more than just show you the end of my shotgun."

Jesse cleared his throat. "Understood, sir."

Hank gave him a brief nod before he started helping him clear the table. Jesse wasn't about to refuse his help. Thankfully, once the table was clear and the dishes in the sink, Hank headed into the living room.

After Jesse got the dishes washed and dried, he figured he'd have to hunt for Liberty. But as soon as he stepped out the back door, he saw her swinging on the rope swing that hung from a big oak tree. It was dark, but the light on the side of the barn illuminated her. With her bare feet pumping and her braids flying, she looked like a little girl.

He moved in front of her and when she sailed toward him, he reached out and tickled the bottoms of her feet. She released a giggle before she swung out of the light and into the darkness. When she came back, she was scowling.

"What are you doing?"

"My sister Adeline used to love for me to tickle her feet when I took her to the park to swing." He reached for her feet again, but she drew them back.

"I don't like to be tickled."

"That giggle said otherwise."

"It was a giggle of surprise."

"Bullshit. Why do you shun all fun, Libby Lou?"

She brought her feet down to the ground and skidded to a stop. "You really are annoying."

He moved closer, stopping in front of her. "And you really are uptight and need to lighten up. I love succeeding as much as you do, but it's okay to take a break every now and then and just have fun."

"I have fun."

"Really? Name one time in the last week that you just had fun."

"Swimming at Cooper Springs."

He lifted his eyebrows. "Are you saying you had fun with me at Cooper Springs, Liberty Holiday?"

She realized her mistake and quickly tried to backpedal. "I enjoyed swimming. It had nothing to do with you."

He grinned. "Liar. You wouldn't have liked it half as much if I hadn't been there to challenge you." He covered her hands on the rope with his and leaned closer, his lips inches from hers. "You like the thrill of competition. It's not just fun. It gets your heart pumping." He lowered his gaze to her mouth. "Is your heart pumping right now, Lib?"

Her lips parted and when he lifted his gaze, her eyes held the same desire that throbbed inside of him. He knew if he kissed her, she would answer every pull of his lips and every brush of his tongue. His body cried out for that . . . but his gut told him the path to Liberty's bed had to be taken slow, not rushed.

He removed her hands from the ropes and pulled her to her feet. When she was standing, he took her place on the wooden seat and tugged her onto his lap before pushing off.

"What are you doing, Jesse Cates?" she hollered.

"You better stop wiggling or you're going to slip right off my lap and bust your butt . . . or possibly your head."

She stopped wiggling and looped her arms around his neck and held on tightly. He liked Liberty holding on to him much more than he should. "These ropes are old, you fool. With your added weight, we're both likely to bust our heads."

He looked down at her stunningly beautiful features and smiled as he pumped higher into the starry sky. "Then I guess we'll fall together."

Chapter Eleven

LIBERTY WOKE THE next morning feeling slightly disoriented. She stared at the bright sunlight shining in through the crack of the curtains for a second before she realized what was wrong.

She'd slept through the night.

Last night, she'd climbed into bed and fallen right to sleep. She hadn't counted sheep. She hadn't worried about losing the ranch or the list of things she needed to get done when she got back to Houston. She'd just conked out and slept through the entire night. Since she couldn't remember the last time that had happened, it freaked her out.

She had to be coming down with something.

She felt her forehead, but she didn't feel hot. Nor did she have a stomachache or a headache. In fact, she felt better and more energized than she had in a long time. She felt like she could run a marathon. Or maybe a triathlon. She tried to figure out what she had done differently last night than all the sleepless nights before.

Only one word popped into her head.

Jesse.

The man was cocky and annoying, but he was also entertaining. She had laughed more last night than she had laughed in a long time. He had swung them so high in the swing that she hadn't been able to stop shrieking with glee. Once he'd brought the swing to a stop, he twisted the ropes and whirled them around like a top. She'd giggled so hard she'd almost peed her pants.

When they had stopped spinning, she should have gotten off his lap. But she hadn't. She had just sat there with her arms looped around his neck, wishing he would kiss her. She'd figured that one little ol' kiss wouldn't hurt anything. She could kiss him and not go to bed with him.

But he hadn't kissed her.

Instead, he had looked up into the branches of the old oak tree and challenged her to a tree-climbing contest. She had taken him up on the challenge, of course, and quickly figured out that climbing the tree had been much easier when she was a kid. But she'd done it and taunted Jesse from the high branch she sat on. He'd taken off his boots and easily scaled the tree and joined her, whereupon they had gotten into a heated verbal battle on who had done it quicker.

Even that had made her laugh.

By the time they climbed down and he walked her back to the house, with his boots dangling from one hand and the other resting on the small of her back, she hadn't been able to stop smiling. She had even invited him to sit on the porch.

He had declined, then hopped in his obnoxious truck and left.

Without trying to kiss her once.

Her eyes narrowed on the shaft of light shining in through the opening in the curtains.

What was the man up to? If he was trying to seduce her, he was doing a piss-poor job.

The thought had her angry all over again. But this time at herself.

"What are you thinking, Liberty Holiday? You should be thankful he's not trying to seduce you, instead of lying here wishing he had. You have a bet to win. And you damn well aren't going to win it by kissing Jesse."

She jumped out of bed and headed into the bathroom to shower.

Once she was dressed, she went downstairs to discover that everyone was gone. In the kitchen, she spied the note on the refrigerator from her mama, reminding her about Daddy's heart specialist appointment in Austin and Mimi's book club meeting in town. Mimi had even taken Tay-Tay with her.

Which meant Liberty was alone.

Being alone wasn't something Liberty was used to. As a twin, she'd had company even in the womb. She quickly tried calling Belle. When her sister didn't answer, she tried calling her other four sisters. Not one answered. Obviously, everyone had something to do this morning but her.

She sighed and flopped down in a kitchen chair. "So much for being ready to win a triathlon." She tapped her phone and started looking at ideas on Pinterest for a five-year-old girl's birthday party. She had just started making a list of things she needed when the doorbell rang.

She sprang up like a jack-in-the-box. Hopefully, it was someone from the Wi-Fi company. But when she opened the door, there was no one there. A large box sat on the doormat and a FedEx truck was heading down the road in a cloud of dust.

She picked up the box and carried it inside. She set it on the kitchen counter before looking to see who it was addressed to. Libby Lou Holiday. Besides Mimi, there was only one person who called her that.

Taking a knife from a drawer, she opened the box. Inside, she found three other boxes. She opened the first one and discovered a box of mocha chocolate muffins from some online specialty bakery. The second box had a straw cowboy hat with a feather sticking in its brim. And the box on the bottom held a pair of brand-new brown roper boots.

The ornery man hadn't gotten her one thing she'd asked for. And yet, she ended up liking everything he'd picked out. The muffins were almost as good as Sheryl Ann's. The cowboy hat looked adorable on. And the boots fit her to perfection with just enough give.

Of course, she couldn't keep them. Well, maybe the muffins since she'd already eaten one. But the hat and the boots she had to return . . . after she did a little teasing. She picked up her phone and tapped the screen.

What happened to the diamonds and Ferragamos?

She only had to wait a moment for the reply.

Those requests were from Liberty Holiday, tough businesswoman. My gifts are for Libby Lou, fun-lovin' country gal.

She laughed as she texted back. Fun-lovin' country gals like diamonds and designer heels too.

He replied right away. But this fun-lovin' country boy likes you in hats and boots.

Thank you, but I can't accept them. At least not the boots and hat. I ate a muffin.

Well, that's a shame because I got them on sale and they're nonrefundable. I guess I'll have to find another fun-lovin' country gal to give them to.

She didn't know what bothered her most: another woman getting the cute hat and comfy boots or Jesse giving them to her.

Fine. If you can't return them, I'll keep them. Thank you.

You're welcome.

She should leave it at that, but she was too starved for company to listen to logical thinking.

What are you doing?

Just answering emails. You?

Planning a little girl's birthday party.

Sounds about as exciting as answering emails. Only a second later another text came in. Would a fun-lovin' country girl want to go on a picnic at Cooper Springs?

The last thing she needed to do if she wanted

to win the bet was be alone with Jesse. But when she answered, it wasn't to decline.

With swimsuits?

Only if you insist.

I insist.

Party pooper. I'll pick you up at noon. Bring the muffins.

I'm not sharing my muffins.

Then I won't share my tacos.

Tito's?

Where else would I get tacos in Wilder?

Fine, I'll share my muffins. Two shredded pork with extra spicy salsa.

Oh, you can bet that I'll bring the extra spice, darlin'.

It seemed that the seduction was about to begin.

Why that made Liberty smile, she didn't know.

Three hours later, she was sitting cross-legged on the blanket she'd brought to Cooper Springs enjoying the best tacos in Texas and tapping notes on her phone. She'd come up with some ideas for Pip's party on the way to Cooper Springs and she wanted to jot them down before she forgot them.

Jesse was stretched out next to her with his eyes closed. It was hard to keep her focus when so much naked skin was on display. The only thing he wore was a pair of shark-print swim trunks that rode so low on his six-pack stomach she could see the white skin bordering his tan line. A thin line of reddish hair ran from the dark shadow of his belly button under the waistband of his trunks. Trunks that didn't leave much to the imagination. She could see the outline of his—

"Are you eyeballing my taco?"

Her gaze flashed up to his face. His eyes were closed, but he must have seen her gawking at his body. She quickly came up with an excuse. "I'm just concerned you're going to get burned. Did you put on sunscreen?"

"Yes, ma'am, but I'm also one of those rare redheads who doesn't burn easily."

Her gaze returned to his chest and the question popped out before she could stop it. "Do you work out shirtless?" He still didn't open his eyes, but a smirk tickled the corners of his mouth. She tried to cover her blooper. "I'm just asking because your chest is tanned and . . ."

"And so muscular it hurts your eyes?"

She rolled her eyes and went back to making her list. "Never mind."

He sat up, hooking his arms over his bent knees. "I work out at a gym when I can, but usually with a shirt on. I only go without a shirt when I'm doing yard work."

"Yard work? You have a yard?"

"No. But Corbin's trailer does and it's filled with weeds. Or it used to be."

She started at him. "Corbin's trailer? You're staying out at Corbin's uncle's place?"

"It's Corbin's now. So I thought I'd help him clean it up. It's in pretty rough shape."

"Why would he want to clean it up? He can't be planning on keeping it."

"Why not?"

"Because I saw it when his uncle owned it and it was pathetic then. I'm sure it's even more so now. And I'm sure he has a nicer home or apartment."

"He does." Jesse shrugged. "But maybe he wants to keep his uncle's place because of the memories."

Liberty snorted. "Not likely. His uncle wasn't what you would call a good memory maker. The only memories I have of him are coming drunk to the high school games and making scenes or getting in arguments with people in town or my daddy. He was an angry man who never had a kind word to say to anyone. Especially poor Corbin. I'm surprised Corbin didn't tell you."

Jesse's eyes held a sadness Liberty had never seen before. "No. He never mentioned it."

That wasn't so strange. The men she knew struggled to talk about anything but business, sports, or ranching. She started to go back to her list when Jesse reached over and took her phone.

"Hey! Give that back."

He shook his head. "I didn't invite you on a picnic so I could sit here and watch you tap away on your phone."

"You weren't sitting. You were lying." She held out a hand. "Give it back."

He lifted his eyebrows. "Or what?"

"Or I'm going to make you pay."

His eyes twinkled. "Really? Then make me pay, Libby Lou."

She hesitated for only a second before she lunged for her phone. But he was much faster and moved it out of her reach . . . and kept moving it out of her reach as she kept trying to grab it. Finally she got so angry, she growled and tackled him back to the blanket. A wrestling match ensued. Not that Jesse did much wrestling. He mostly just lay there, laughing, as he moved his arm to keep her phone just out of her reach.

"I'm warning you, Jesse Cates, if you don't give me back my phone—"

He easily rolled her over until he was on top.

Just like that, she forgot all about her phone. All she could think about was the way her body felt tucked beneath all those muscles.

She had never liked men being on top. It made her feel trapped. But with Jesse, she didn't feel trapped. She felt . . . safe. Like being wrapped in her great-grandma's quilt. Except instead of patched material, the blanket was made of hard muscle and a rapidly thumping heart. As she looked into his soft brown eyes, she felt no need to be on top. No need to take control.

"Or you'll do what, Libby Lou?" he said in a voice that was husky and sexy.

Only one thing popped into her mind.

As it turned out, she took control after all.

She slid her hands over the broad width of his shoulders, enjoying the feel of his sun-toasted skin, before she glided them up the corded muscles of his neck and cradled his whiskered jaw. "Or this." She kissed him.

As soon as their mouths collided, she realized how much she had longed for this. She felt ravenous and Jesse was the only one who could feed the hunger inside her. But instead of joining in on her frenzied kiss, he drew back and whispered against her lips.

"Slow down, Libby. There's no rush." He sipped at her mouth a few times before he deepened the kiss, teaching her the difference between a rushed devouring and a slow, unhurried mating of lips and tongues. He didn't just taste her. He savored her, turning her into a puddle of want and need.

He wanted her too. She could feel him growing hard against the top of her leg. She shifted to get that hardness exactly where she wanted it. When he rubbed his erection against the aching spot, she groaned with the pleasure it ignited.

She was losing the bet. Her mind knew this. But her body didn't seem to care. It wanted more. She opened her legs as he continued to rock against her. When he wasn't moving fast enough, she slipped her hands to his butt to urge him on. He chuckled against her lips before he followed her instruction, rubbing his hard length against her until the pulsing ache between her legs turned into an explosive release.

As she dug her fingers into his butt cheeks and arched into him, he slowed his movements and eased her down from her orgasm with feather-soft kisses and words of encouragement.

"That's it, Lib. Ride it out, baby."

She wilted down to the blanket and sighed, completely spent and relaxed . . . for about three seconds. Then her mind plopped back into her head and she realized what she'd done.

She shoved him off and scrambled to her feet. "If you think for one second that you've won the bet, Jesse Cates, you can think again. Our bet was about you getting me in bed and that means sex. What we just had wasn't sex. That was just me reaching orgasm by myself."

He rested back on his forearms, his red hair mussed, and his brown eyes hazed with desire. "Well, there's no doubt, darlin', that you were the only one who had an orgasm." He glanced down at the front of his swim trunks. The thin waterproof fabric did nothing to disguise his large erection. "But I think I had a little something to do with it."

She couldn't argue. "Fine. You had something to do with it. But it wasn't sex."

He rolled to his feet and shrugged. "Then I guess I'll have to up my game." He started toward her and she held up a hand.

"Now just because I let you give me an orgasm that doesn't mean—" Before she could finish, he walked right past her and dove into the springs. He rose up out of the water with a loud hoot and a wide smile.

"Come on in, Libby Lou. The water feels great!"

After what had just happened, she had no desire to test her willpower again. "No, thank you, I need to get back to my party planning." She turned to the blanket and froze. "Where's my phone?" She looked back at him. "Don't you dare tell me that you took it into the springs."

"Now would I do something like that when I know how much you love your phone?"

"Then where is it?"

"I'll be happy to tell you if you can beat me at

a race." He winked. "Ready, set , go!" He took off swimming for the opposite shore. Liberty had no choice but to slip off her cover-up and dive into the water. He still beat her by a good ten yards.

But she wasn't mad. She was finding it harder and harder to stay mad at Jesse.

She laughed as she splashed him with water. "Then I guess we're even."

He gave her a heated look. "Oh, no, Libby Lou. We're not even. It's now one orgasm to none. But just to be clear, I don't mind at all if you go up by two . . . or three."

It took every ounce of willpower she had to turn from the steamy promise in those eyes and swim for shore.

Chapter Twelve

"OPEN UP YOUR mouth. I need to check your teeth and see if you have any tartar."

Jesse opened his mouth wide and the little dark-haired girl in the white lab coat with *Veterinarian Pippin* embroidered on the pocket peeked into his mouth. Her entire face scrunched up in a serious, intent look. She'd been given the right nickname. The five-year-old was a pip.

"Yep, you have tartar, alright." She leaned closer. "I can see it on your back tooths. And tartar can lead to heart failure."

Jesse closed his mouth. "Really?"

Pip nodded sagely. "Especially in old dogs."

Jesse stared at her. "Old dogs?"

"I can tell by your tooths that you are at least ten years old. Which makes you seventy in people years."

"Hey, kid, I'm not seventy."

Pip reached up and scratched the floppy ear that was attached to the dog costume Jesse wore. "It's okay, boy. With a little tooth-cleaning, you'll still have a few good years left."

"That's good to know," he said dryly. "But if you think you're cleaning my teeth, Doctor Pip, you got another think coming."

"Of course I'm not cleaning your teeth." She turned to the little freckled-face girl standing behind her. "My assistant, Didi, will do it."

Didi shook her head. "My mama doesn't like me sticking my hands in people's germy mouths."

"Smart mama," Jesse said. "Now if you're done with your examination, Doc." He went to get up, but Pip pushed him right back down into the chair.

"Nope, I haven't checked for worms."

Jesse swallowed hard. "Worms?"

It wasn't until much later that Jesse was able to escape Pip's veterinarian chair of torture. But as soon as he did, he was bombarded with little five-year-old girls hugging his legs and pulling on his tail and pleading with "the big fuzzy dog" to give them piggyback rides. Jesse had always been a sucker for cute little girls. His sister Adeline had completely wrapped him around her little finger.

Thankfully, before his fur became too matted by sticky fingers and his back gave out, Liberty hollered.

"Birthday cake time!"

The little girls raced off, squealing with delight, while Jesse followed much more slowly. As he came around the corner of the blow-up bouncy house, he saw Liberty lighting the candles on a cake that was decorated with animal paw prints on the side and a toy stereoscope and shot syringe on top.

He should be pissed at her. She was the reason he was wearing a silly dog costume with floppy ears and a long tail he kept tripping over. Of course, it was his own fault. He shouldn't have agreed to a bet where winner chooses the forfeit. Nor should he have gotten so distracted by the way Liberty's wet swimming suit had ridden up one butt cheek that he didn't care about winning the race to his truck and instead lagged behind enjoying the view.

He smiled. And damned if the view hadn't been worth wearing a sweltering dog costume. That and the way she laughed every time she saw him in the costume. Even now, when her gaze lifted and those green eyes landed on him, she smiled so brightly it took his breath away.

Be careful, Jess.

The warning had popped into his head frequently in the last few days. Each time, he reasoned with his mind. He liked Liberty. He liked her a lot. But that's all it was. He enjoyed being around her, but only because they were so much alike. They were both driven and competitive. They were both business minded. And they both weren't interested in getting married and starting a family. She had told him so herself.

Which was why there was no reason Jesse needed to be careful. Neither one of them wanted to end up on a couch for family movie night. In fact, today, he'd gotten the distinct feeling Liberty didn't like kids. She had done a great job at pulling the party together. She'd been the perfect hostess, making sure both the kids and adults were having a good time and had plenty to eat and drink. But there was a look she got in her eyes whenever she was around the little girls. A terrified look like she couldn't get away fast enough.

"Would you mind if I took a picture of you holding my baby?"

He turned and saw a woman standing there holding a blanket-wrapped bundle.

"Hi. I'm Tammy Sue. You must be Jesse Cates, Liberty's new beau."

Jesse blinked. "Beau? Umm . . . well, I don't know if I'd call myself—"

Tammy Sue cut him off before he could continue. "When I heard she was dating Corbin Whitlock's friend, I was more than a little worried—we all know what a scoundrel he is. And I've known Liberty ever since she was born. I want her to get the kind of man who will do right by her. Not some lowlife drifter who is only interested in getting into her panties. But after today, I realize just what kind of man you are. My husband would never—ever—dress up in a ridiculous dog outfit for me." Her eyes narrowed. "Even though I've given him three kids and the best years of my life."

Jesse wasn't sure what to say to that. So he just nodded, which caused his floppy ears to swing and Tammy Sue to smile.

"Just so cute." She handed him the bundle.

Since he had babysat Adeline when she was a baby, he had no fear of holding infants. Although once he accepted the bundle, he grew a little concerned. The kid was the size of a football.

"He's just a month old," Tammy Sue said. "Isn't he the sweetest nugget?"

Nugget was accurate. Jesse pinned on a smile hoping Tammy would quickly snap the picture and take her tiny son back. But as soon as she lifted her phone, bloodcurdling screams came from the bounce house.

Tammy Sue's eyes widened. "I'll be right back. Thomas! Heather! Mama's comin'!"

Jesse started to give her the baby back, but then realized she couldn't very well climb into the bounce house with a newborn. A newborn who started fussing as if he knew his mother was gone.

Jesse bounced him. "It's okay, sport. Mama will be back in just a second."

Unfortunately, when Mama crawled out of the bounce house it was with two toddlers who looked like they had been in fight club. The girl had scratches on her arms and the boy had a bite mark on his cheek. They were both still screaming bloody murder.

"I'm sorry," Tammy Sue said. "Would you mind watching Douglas while I take care of these two ornery kids?" She didn't wait for a reply as she dragged her two screaming kids toward the house.

"What in the world is going on?" Liberty came hurrying up. As soon as Jesse turned to her, she burst out laughing.

"I'm glad you're so amused. Here. Your turn." He handed her Douglas.

"What's this?" She giggled. "Did one of the girls

give the big ol' fuzzy dog their doll to babysit?" Douglas released a fussy *wahhh* and Liberty's smile faded. She glanced down at the baby and all color drained from her face.

Like all color.

"Liberty?" He reached out and took her arm. "Are you okay?"

She lifted her eyes to him. There was the fear again. But also a deep pain that cut right through him. "Take it . . . please."

As soon as he took the baby from her arms, she turned and headed around the bounce house. He wanted to go after her, but Douglas started crying even louder and he figured he needed to deal with one upset person at a time. He shifted the baby to his shoulder and patted his back as he walked to the house. Once the baby was with his mama, Jesse went in search of Liberty.

He found her sitting on the ground behind the bounce house. He sat down next to her, stretching out his legs and crossing his dog paws in an attempt to get her to laugh. She didn't.

"You okay?" he asked.

"I'm fine. I just needed a little break."

"Yeah. I forgot how tiring kids' birthday parties are." He shot her a glance. "Especially when you're the life of the party." He shook his floppy ears and woofed.

A smile tipped the corner of her mouth. "You were. Pip wants to keep you—even though you have tartar and worms." She glanced at him. "Exactly how did she find out you had worms?"

"She had to check out my fecal sample." When

Liberty's eyes widened, he laughed. "It was a Tootsie Roll she dissected with a pair of kid's scissors." He shook his head. "All I can say is the kid is going to make a great vet. And I don't think she'll ever forget this party. Good job, Libby Lou." He hesitated. "Especially when you're scared to death of kids."

"I'm not scared of kids."

"Then you want to explain the terrified look you've had the entire party and the panic attack when I handed you Douglas?"

He thought she would deny her reactions. Instead, she spoke in a soft whisper he could barely hear. "I can't have kids. I have endometriosis and it's left a lot of scar tissue on my ovaries."

Everything fell into place. She wasn't scared of kids. She was scared that she'd never have her own. Which confused him.

"I thought you weren't interested in having kids."

"I thought I wasn't. But now that it's unlikely I can get pregnant . . ." She let the sentence drift off, but he understood. It was one thing to make that decision for yourself and another to have it taken from you.

He pulled the paws off his hands and drew her into his arms. He didn't say anything. He didn't know what to say. Sorry didn't seem like enough. So he just held her. She didn't sob or cry like most women would have. She just burrowed into the fake fur of his costume and clung to him as if he were a lifeline. Since Liberty was not a clinger, it broke his heart just as much as her tears.

After a while, he spoke. "My adoptive mama, Shirlene, couldn't have kids. She tried for years and years and finally just gave up. Then four ornery foster kids showed up on her doorstep. I guess God had a plan for her all along. She said she just wished He had clued her in on it a little sooner so she wouldn't have wasted all that money on fertility doctors and pregnancy tests."

He felt more than heard Liberty's chuckle. "Your mama sounds like a fun woman."

"You have no idea. She believes in living life to the fullest." He stroked her hair, loving the way it felt sliding through his fingers. "You remind me of her."

She glanced up at him. He could lose himself in those green eyes. "I thought you said I didn't know how to let go and just have fun."

"You're getting better at it."

She was. There was a light in her eyes that hadn't been there before. A light that drew him much more than any sexual chemistry between them. She tried to act like a tough businesswoman who could handle a sexual relationship with no strings and no attachments—a realist who knew that happily-ever-afters weren't for everyone. But he realized now that it was all a façade.

Liberty Holiday *did* believe in happily-ever-after. How could she not when she'd grown up in a big farmhouse with a loving family? She hadn't lived the harsh reality Jesse had lived. She hadn't had to install a shield for her heart to keep it safe.

Jesse could feel that shield going up right now. But before it was completely in place, he couldn't stop himself from taking one last kiss. Her sweet lips melted beneath his and for a second—just a second—he let himself feel everything he was starting to feel for this woman. All the emotions he kept so tightly under lock and key.

Then he drew back and spoke the words that needed to be spoken. Not only to shield him from pain, but also to shield Liberty.

"You won. I'm going to convince Corbin to stop the foreclosure proceedings."

Her eyes registered surprise before they narrowed. "Oh, you're good, Jesse Cates. You're extremely good. This is where you expect me to fall head over boots into bed with you."

He glanced around. "Well, it might be risky. But if you're willing to take the chance, darlin', I am too." He went to pull her back into his arms, but, as he knew she would, she slapped his hands away."

"I wasn't talking about here, you ingrate. The only reason you'd ever lose a bet is if you think it will ultimately get you what you want. Well, you're out of luck this time. I'm not falling for your man-with-a-golden-heart act. But a man's word is a man's word. Since you already declared yourself the loser, there's no reneging."

He didn't have to try to conjure up a look of disappointment. He was disappointed—disappointed in himself for not being brave enough to take a chance. He knew it wouldn't be long before a much braver man than he came along and loved Liberty the way she deserved to be loved. With his entire heart. A heart that wasn't damaged.

Before he could think of some witty reply, Pip appeared with her horde of friends trailing behind her. Her eyes lit up when she saw him. "There you are, Fluffy! Come on, we're going into the bouncy house." She grabbed his hand and tried to tug him to his feet.

He looked at Liberty for help, but she just grinned and handed him his paws. "You can't disappoint the birthday girl, Fluffy."

He sighed and put on his paws before he got to his feet. He held out a paw to Liberty. "If I'm going, you're going."

"Oh, no, I'm not getting in that thing."

"Afraid Fluffy can out bounce you?"

Her eyes narrowed and she stood without his help. "Not in this lifetime." She headed around the bounce house. "Come on, girls. Let's show this dog how to bounce."

He followed behind, but at a slower pace.

Damn, he was going to miss her.

Chapter Thirteen

～

THE HOLIDAY SECRET Sisterhood had started years ago when the Holiday sisters were just kids. The meetings took place at least once a month, either in person or by Zoom, depending on where all the sisters were at the time.

Tonight, it was on Zoom.

Noelle was in Dallas standing at a counter in what looked like one of her culinary classrooms, whisking something in a bowl. Hallie was in the brewery room of the brewery she worked at in Austin. Belle was at their office in Houston, the picture she'd had blown up of the Holiday Ranch directly behind her. Cloe was cozied up on a couch at the Remington Ranch. Sweetie was sitting on the porch of the quaint house she shared with Decker.

Liberty would have loved to be sitting in the swing on her parents' porch. But since there was still no Wi-Fi at the ranch and she'd had a craving for Bobby Jay's baby back ribs and twofer margaritas, she'd come to the Hellhole for dinner.

It certainly had nothing to do with hoping to run into a cocky cowboy.

She glanced around the restaurant and bar for what felt like the hundredth time while she tried to stay focused on the conversation. It seemed Noelle had met the love of her life. While she measured ingredients and whisked them into whatever she was making, she was expounding on her new boyfriend's many virtues. Liberty might be more interested in the conversation if her littlest sister hadn't found the love of her life every other week.

"I'm telling y'all, Luc is the one," Noelle said. "He's not only a hot Frenchman with a dreamy accent and a slew of awards for his pastries, but he's also funny and polite and not at all arrogant . . . like some people I know."

All the sisters knew she wasn't talking about some people. She was talking about one person. Her archenemy, Casey Remington, Rome's little brother. The two had been at each other's throats since kindergarten. Something Liberty had always found amusing.

Tonight, she was too preoccupied to be amused.

She glanced around the bar again and scowled when she didn't spot a rodeo bum with strawberry-blond hair and an impish smile. She hated to admit it, but she missed that impish smile. She hadn't seen hide nor hair of it since Pip's party. The morning after the party, he'd picked up Tay-Tay while she'd been visiting Cloe and hadn't been back to the ranch since. Nor had he stopped by Nothin' But Muffins and she'd been there every morning for the last week. Nor had he shown up at Cooper Springs while she was taking her afternoon and nighttime swims.

She thought about texting him, but she flat-out refused to be one of those women who fired off a hundred texts to a man who had ghosted her.

That's exactly what Jesse had done. He had backed out of the bet and cut her off without any explanation.

Of course, she didn't need one. She already knew.

She'd let down her guard and showed him the needy woman beneath the tough businesswoman. The woman who wanted children and a family—even though she said she didn't.

It was the dog suit that had done it.

While most men wouldn't have been caught dead in a fuzzy dog suit, Jesse had not only worn it, but also embraced the part. The kids had adored him and so had their parents. Everyone at the birthday party had commented how great he was with children.

It had made her want something she couldn't have.

Not just kids, but Jesse.

He was the type of person who made people feel happy to be alive. At least that's how he'd made Liberty feel. He'd made her feel more alive than she'd felt in years. She'd laughed more, enjoyed life more, and slept more. Now she was back to being stressed, bored, and not sleeping.

And it was annoying. Damn annoying.

She didn't need Jesse Cates to live life to the fullest. She could live quite nicely without him.

She pushed him from her mind and cut into Noelle's fawning over Luc. "I'm sure Luc is amazing, Elle, and I'm real happy for you. But I didn't call this meeting to talk about our love lives. I called it to tell y'all that Jesse has agreed to convince Corbin to stop the foreclosure proceedings."

She thought her sisters would look relieved. She was surprised when they didn't.

"What exactly did you have to do to get him to agree?" Sweetie asked.

"I was wondering the same thing," Cloe said.

Liberty didn't believe in beating around the bush. "If you're asking me if I had sex with him, the answer is no."

"Are you planning on having sex with him?" Cloe asked.

She didn't know where the brick of disappointment in her stomach came from. "Absolutely not."

"But you kissed him twice," Hallie said.

Liberty sent both Cloe and Sweetie glares. "You told?"

"You should have told us," Noelle said as she viciously whisked. "That's just part of the Secret Sisterhood oath we took. No secrets from sisters. Especially juicy secrets." She stopped whisking and leaned closer to her screen. "So have you kissed him again?"

"Once." Not that anyone would call what she and Jesse had done at Cooper Springs just a kiss.

For the past few nights, when she did finally fall asleep, she dreamed about the feel of Jesse's hard body rocking against her.

"Did something else come with that kiss?" Hallie asked. "Because that's a hot-sex flush if ever I saw one."

Her face grew even warmer and there was a "Nailed it!" from Hallie and a squeal of excitement from Noelle and a gasp of disbelief from Belle—no doubt because Liberty hadn't told her—and a worried sigh from both Cloe and Sweetie.

"We didn't have sex!" Liberty yelled so loudly the people sitting around her stopped talking and stared at her. She stared right back. "What? Haven't you ever heard a grown woman talking about sex before?" They quickly turned away and she looked back at her laptop.

"But you want to have sex with Jesse," Noelle said.

"Yep, she does," Hallie joined in.

Thankfully, Belle came to her rescue. "That's none of our business, Elle and Hal. There are some things sisters should keep to themselves." Liberty couldn't help being surprised. Belle had confided everything to her . . . hadn't she? "Now let's get back to the issue at hand." Belle continued. "Do you think Jesse can convince Corbin to let Rome pay off the loan?"

Liberty didn't even hesitate to answer. Jesse might have ghosted her, but he wasn't the type of man to renege on his word.

"Yes. The man is extremely persuasive." Her sisters all sent her knowing looks and she rolled her eyes. "Moving on. Is there any other issues we need to discuss?"

Cloe held up a photograph. "Does anyone want to see your new niece?" Everyone started talking at once as Cloe moved the blurred ultrasound image closer to the camera. It looked like a tiny withered potato. While Cloe talked about how Rome had cried when he'd seen the ultra sound of his daughter, Liberty tried to keep a smile on her face and not give in to the hollow feeling in the pit of her stomach.

It was a losing battle.

It seemed that talking to Jesse the other day at the party had opened up the internal safe Liberty had locked all her secret desires in. Now there was no more pretending that she didn't want children or a husband who cried over ultrasound images. But very few men would be willing to get into a relationship with a woman who couldn't have children. Even men like Jesse who acted like they didn't want kids. He might not want kids, but he wouldn't want that choice taken from him.

Maybe that's why he'd ghosted her. Maybe he was completely turned off by the fact she was defective.

The more she thought about him ghosting her all because she couldn't have the kids he didn't even want, the madder she got . . . and the more she downed the two margaritas the barmaid had brought her.

By the time she was finished Zooming with her sisters, both of her twofer margaritas were gone and she was madder than a wet hen. Or possibly a tipsy hen. She fired off a quick text to her ghost and pushed send, then jumped up from her chair and yelled, "Who wants to dance!"

A lot of people took her up on the offer—men and women. She discovered why once she was out on the dance floor. It seemed word had gotten out about Pip's party and now everyone wanted Liberty to plan their events.

"So I'm in a bit of a pickle," Mayor Deidre Sims said as she whirled Liberty under her arm flab, then continued the jaunty polka they were doing. "Carol Hyde always takes care of the Memorial and Fourth of July activities, but after hip-replacement surgery, she just can't do it." The mayor leaned in closer. "And just between you and me, Carol never did have a flair for decorations. Last year, she decorated the Miss Soybean float with orange flowers. Not red, white, and blue for Fourth of July. Not white, pink, or purple for the soybean flowers. Orange. I have never had so many hate emails in all my born days."

Liberty giggled, which proved how drunk she was. She did not giggle.

"I know you have a flair with decorations," the mayor continued. "When you were in high school, I knew I could count on you and your sister to make every homecoming and prom look like the set of a teen movie." Mayor Sims had been the principal of the high school before she had been elected mayor. Which was why Liberty couldn't tell her no.

That and the warm glow in her belly from the margaritas.

"I'd be honored to be in charge of decorations and fes-tible—fe-sis—activities for the Memorial and Fourth of July celebrations."

"Great!" The mayor handed her off to Danny Bell, who told her all about his daughter who wanted a fancy wedding on a postman's budget.

By the time she'd danced with what felt like the entire town, she had agreed to help plan two weddings, a twenty-fifth wedding anniversary, a prom proposal for a shy sixteen-year-old, the Memorial Day and Fourth of July celebrations, and a funeral for a beloved hunting dog.

She was now sober and thoroughly pissed at Bobby Jay for making his margaritas so damn strong. Before she got any more jobs, she grabbed her phone and laptop and started for the door. But halfway there, the town bully stopped her.

"Hey there, beautiful." Cob Ritter hooked an arm around her waist. "Where you goin'? The night is still young."

"I'm not in the mood for an idiot tonight, Cob. So before I do what Cloe did last time you accosted her and relocate your balls between your ears, you might want to let me go."

His smile faded and his beady eyes narrowed. "That won't happen again. I've learned the Holiday sisters need a firm hand." He tightened his grip and tugged her so close she couldn't move her legs. "Now, honey, you don't want to hurt the goods before you've gotten a sample, do you?"

Before she could grab the beer bottle sitting on the bar and bust it over Cob's head, a deep voice spoke behind him.

"Let her go."

Liberty peeked over Cob's shoulder and saw Jesse standing there in his crumpled hat. He wasn't wearing his usual cocky smile. He looked pissed. Real pissed. And Liberty wasn't so happy herself.

"Well, if it isn't the Ghost of Jesse Cates."

He didn't reply. His gaze remained narrowed on Cob who had turned around, but still had a firm hold of Liberty's arm. "I said let her go," Jesse repeated.

Cob grinned. "I don't think—" He didn't even get to finish before Jesse punched him in the jaw. Cob released Liberty and wavered on his feet for only a second before his eyes rolled back and he landed in a heap at her feet. Before Liberty could get over her surprise, Jesse took her hand and pulled her toward the door.

Once outside, she jerked free. "I don't need you showing up and playing hero, Jesse Cates. So go on back inside and seduce all the women you want. Isn't that what you're here for? To find an easier woman to get into your bed."

"I'm here because you drunk texted me."

"I did not drunk text you."

He pulled out his phone, tapped it a few times, before he handed it to her. "So you meant to call me an egg testicle jerk?"

She read the text.

Boy was I wrote about you. You're nothing butt

a shellfish egg testicle jerk. Ass far ass I concert you can go straight to Jell-O.

She cringed. Damn autocorrect . . . and Bobby's margaritas. And damn the arrogant cowboy standing in front of her.

She handed his phone back. "I meant every word. Once you found out I wanted kids—or maybe once you found out I couldn't have them, you called off the bet and ran off like an . . . egg testicle jerk!"

His eyes widened. "That had nothing to do with me calling off the bet."

"Then why did you ghost me?"

He opened his mouth, but then closed it. "Come on, I'll drive you home." He went to take her arm, but she pulled back.

"Didn't you hear me? I don't need your help. In fact, I don't need anything from you. I don't need you to go swimming with me. I don't need you to swing with me. I don't need you to climb trees with me." She leaned in closer and got right in his face. "I—Don't—Need—You."

Jesse stared at her for a long moment before he wrapped his arm around her waist and tugged her close. His eyes held a hunger that made her stomach drop and her heart thump and all her breath leave her lungs in one fell swoop.

"Well, that's too bad, darlin'," he said. "Because, this last week, I figured out that I need you."

He kissed her. This kiss wasn't the slow, seductive kind he'd given her out at Cooper Springs. This kiss was hungry and devouring and . . . thought stealing.

Liberty couldn't think. All she could do was feel. What she felt was uncontrollable desire. She didn't care that he'd run off and ghosted her. She didn't care that he would probably run off and ghost her again. All she cared about was that he was here now. Making her feel things she'd never felt before.

When he lifted her into his arms, she hooked her arms around his neck and held on tight as he carried her to his truck. Once there, he put her down and pushed her back against the passenger door, his lips hot and scorching as he kissed his way along her neck.

"Tell me no," he whispered against her skin. "Stop this before it's too late."

Her head lolled back against the truck to give him better access. "You stop it."

He nipped on her neck, sending a shower of sparks through her body, before he drew back. His eyes held desire and pain. "I can't."

She cradled his face in her hands, wanting to soothe that pain. "Then I guess this is happening because I can't stop either." She kissed him.

They stood there exchanging heated kisses until a group of laughing people came out of the bar, then Jesse helped her into his truck. She hadn't liked the obnoxious vehicle until she discovered how well the bench seat worked for a horny woman. Without a console, she could cozy right up next to Jesse and slide her hands over all the muscles she'd only dreamed about touching.

"Lib-by," he groaned as she slipped her hand

inside the shirt she'd just unsnapped and brushed his nipple with her thumb. "Behave."

But she couldn't behave. Not when her body hummed with the need to touch and taste every inch of the man. She cradled his bunched biceps and ran her hands over his thick thigh muscles. She counted his twin stacks of abdominal muscles and cupped the hard slabs of each pec. When they reached the secluded dirt road that led to Corbin's trailer, she finally slid her hand over the bulge beneath his fly.

The truck veered off the road, its big tires rolling over rocks and flattening sagebrush.

"Jesus, woman!" He corrected his steering and got back on the road before glancing at her. "Are you trying to get us killed?"

She smiled as she slid her hand back over his erection. "Am I distracting you, cowboy?"

He closed his eyes and groaned. "I knew you were going to be a hellion the moment I met you."

He gunned the truck and gravel flew. Within seconds, they were pulling into the dirt lot in front of Corbin's beat-up trailer. It looked a lot more pathetic than Liberty remembered. But she barely had time to take in the rusted siding and the cracked windows before Jesse had her on his lap. His smile was evil as he leered at her.

"You teased me, darlin', and now it's time I teased you." His fingers slid beneath her skirt, leaving behind a trail of tingling heat. "I've been wondering just what you have on under this skirt." His hand stopped on her upper thigh, his index finger brushing her skin in tiny circles that made her breath hitch. "I'd bet Liberty Holiday wears tiny little silk designer panties. But Libby Lou wears something more comfortable and country—cotton panties with tiny little hearts. Or maybe flowers."

She held her breath as his hot fingers moved higher, tracing the leg elastic of her panties in a back-and-forth motion that made her heart race. "Shall we see who's sittin' on my lap tonight, darlin'?"

But he didn't pull her panties off to check. Instead, he used just his fingertips and brushed over the front of them, stroking the throbbing spot between her legs.

"Cotton," he whispered in a husky voice. A smile bloomed on his handsome face. "Hey, Libby Lou. I was hoping for you." He leaned in and kissed her slow and deep as he slipped her panties down her legs that were stretched out on the seat. He stopped when he reached the roper boots he'd bought her and drew back from the kiss. "Nice boots, by the way. Now can you lift one so I can get your panties off? I need to have a little more working room."

She didn't know what he meant until her panties were off and he scooted across the seat with her on his lap to the passenger side. Then he turned her facing away from him and tugged her skirt up around her waist.

"There," he whispered in her ear as he spread her legs and hooked them over his knees. "Isn't that better?"

Before she could say that she felt a little exposed, he slid a hand up her inner thigh and proceeded to explore. The feel of his calloused fingers slipping between her moist folds had her groaning aloud as her head dropped back on his shoulder.

"That's it, baby," he whispered. "Just lie back and enjoy."

She did enjoy. She enjoyed every stroke and thrust of his talented fingers. When he had her practically weeping with pleasure, he located her clitoris and strummed it in a back-and-forth rhythm that sent her right over the edge. She lifted her hips and cried out in an embarrassing run-on sentence of cusswords and praise for how good he made her feel.

He *was* talented. He knew exactly what to do to draw out her pleasure until she sagged against him in a limp mass of satisfaction.

Jesse pulled her close and kissed the side of her head. "Now don't get too comfortable, darlin'. I believe I promised you three orgasms and I've always been a man of my word."

Chapter Fourteen

JESSE HAD TRIED to let Liberty go. He'd spent the last three days cooped up in the trailer with an angry Tay-Tay who wasn't happy about coming back to a dinky trailer after getting a peek at what it was like to live in a big ranch house.

But Jesse had not wanted to test fate. So he'd stayed away from town. He'd stayed away from Cooper Springs. He'd stayed away from Holiday Ranch. He hadn't called Liberty, texted her, and had even refused to read her text when he'd gotten it tonight.

Instead, he had played solitaire with an old deck of cards he found in a drawer. He lost every game until he realized the deck was missing the queen of hearts, the five of spades, and the two of diamonds. Then he tried entertaining Tay-Tay with the cat toy Mimi had given her. After disinfecting his scratches, he'd gone to bed.

In the dark with nothing to distract him, his phone had whispered to him.

Just read the text. You don't have to answer it.

He'd read it and the jumbled mess of words had made him laugh . . . and worry. So he'd texted her back. When she didn't answer, he called her. When she still didn't answer, he'd called the Holiday Ranch and talked to Darla who had told him Liberty's whereabouts. The thought of her being drunk at a bar with a bunch of horny cowboys had sent him running for his truck. Once he'd walked into the Hellhole and seen her in another man's arms, his oath to stay away from her had completely dissolved.

All he'd felt was unmitigated jealousy and anger. How dare another man touch what was his?

Except she wasn't his.

Liberty would never belong to any man. But that didn't stop him from wishing she was . . . or from bringing her home when he knew it was a mistake.

Now here he stood in the bedroom of Corbin's trailer looking down at the most beautiful woman he'd ever met in his life lying naked on the mattress and he didn't regret reneging on his oath to stay away from her. Not for one second. He had told her that he needed her, but the ache he felt inside was so much more than need. She had become an all-consuming necessity. Like air and water.

All he could hope for was that if he glutted himself on her, the feeling would go away.

"Are you just going to stand there staring, cowboy?" she said in a husky voice that made him harder than he already was. Her eyes trailed over his naked body before they settled on his flagrant erection. "Or are you going to make good on your claim?"

"Oh, I'm going to give you that third orgasm, darlin'. But first I want to look my fill." His gaze slid over every inch of her body from the tip of her toes that were surprisingly nail polish free to the ends of her hair that was spread out on his pillow like raven's wings.

She wasn't a curvy woman. Her breasts weren't large or her hips full. And yet, she had a sex appeal that took his breath away. Maybe it was her long, lean legs that seemed to go on forever. Or her small breasts that rested on her rib cage like two perfect scoops of vanilla ice cream topped with plump ripe raspberries. Or the sweet spot shadowed by her toned thighs.

Most women he dated, shaved completely or had a thin strip of pubic hair. But Liberty wasn't most women. Like a small black velvet gift box, neatly trimmed dark hair hid the treasure he desired most.

Unable to wait to open the gift a second longer, he knelt on the mattress and picked up her foot. He kissed the high arch and all five unpainted toes before he lowered it and spread her legs.

The sight of her glistening center took his breath away. He didn't hesitate to lower his head. As he intimately kissed her with lips and tongue, he watched her face to gauge what she liked best. When he found the right tempo of tongue flicks, he gloried in the sight of her coming apart. She held nothing back. She cussed. She moaned. She gripped the sheets in tight fists. She tightened her thighs on his head as if she wasn't ever going to let him go.

He would have gladly stayed there forever. But she finally came down from her orgasm and her eyes opened and her green-eyed gaze found him.

"Get inside me," she whispered.

He followed her order. Once he had a condom on, he slipped inside her still-clenching sheath. Damn, it was a perfect fit. He had to count to twenty and breathe deeply to keep from coming right then and there.

Then she went and ruined his composure by hooking those long legs around his hips, tipping her pelvis, and taking him even deeper into her heavenly warmth.

"Jesse," she said his name in a half moan half groan that dissolved the last of his restrain as a tidal wave of need and emotions consumed him.

There was no more holding back. No more hiding from the things this woman made him feel. She had stripped away his shield, leaving all his emotions completely exposed, and there wasn't anything he could do about it.

"Damn you." He thrust deep. "Damn you."

She hooked her arms around his shoulders and met his next thrust with fire in her green eyes. "No, damn you, Jesse Cates. Damn you to hell and back."

She took him to hell and back. She took him into a fiery inferno that burned right through his soul. When he thought he couldn't take one second more, she pulled him out of the flames and thrust him straight into heaven.

As his orgasm hit, he chanted her name over and over again.

"Lib. Lib. Lib."

He came back to earth to find her smiling up at him. "That's my name, darlin', don't wear it out."

For once, he didn't have a clever retort. He was too blown away by what had just happened. He knew what sex was and this hadn't been it. He didn't know what it had been, but it hadn't been sex. And once again, he was scared shitless.

Without saying a word, he got out of bed and headed into the bathroom. After disposing of the condom, he stood in front of the sink and stared at his reflection. His face was pale and his eyes terrified.

"I take it you're not a cuddler after sex."

He turned to see Liberty standing in the doorway completely dressed. He knew he should say something, but he didn't know what. So he just shook his head.

She studied him with those intense green eyes for a long moment before she shrugged. "Me either. I need a ride back to my car."

Once they were on their way back to the Hellhole, he tried to apologize for his weird behavior. "Look, Libby, I'm sorry. I'm not good at . . ." He let the sentence drift off because he didn't know what this was. If it wasn't casual sex, what was it?

She held up a hand. "You don't have to apologize, Jesse. I'm a big girl who can handle a one-night stand."

He should be happy she wasn't making any demands or expecting more than he could give.

Except he wasn't happy. He felt angry and confused . . . and needy. One night hadn't been enough to satisfy that need. He wanted more. He wanted more of her body and her mind and her challenges and her laughter. And yet, he couldn't bring himself to say it. All he could do was sit there like a pathetic fool and stare out the windshield.

When they got to the Hellhole, the parking lot was completely empty except for her SUV. He pulled next to it and then opened his door, intending to get out and go around to help her out. But she got out and was in her car before he could even make it around the front of his truck. She didn't wave or look at him once as she pulled away.

"Dammit!" He hit the side of his truck with his fist. He didn't care that it hurt like hell or left a dent. He hit it again and cussed a blue streak, but it didn't ease the sinking feeling in the pit of his stomach. He figured if he didn't want to break his hand and ruin his truck, he needed to get a grip.

There was only one person who could soothe him when his emotions got to be too much.

He pulled out his cellphone. He didn't even think about the time until he heard Shirlene's groggy, concerned voice.

"Jesse, honey, what's wrong? Are you okay? Are you injured? Sick? Speak to me, baby."

"I'm fine, Shirl. I shouldn't have called so late."

"Nonsense. You can call me anytime day or night."

"Like hell he can!" Billy's muffled voice came

through the receiver. "If he's not sick, injured, or in jail, he needs to call at a decent hour."

"Now, don't you pay any attention to Billy, honey. You know the man gets grumpy if you wake him up. What's going on?"

He lied. "I just needed to hear your voice."

There was a long pause. "Well, that's real sweet, sugar. It's nice to hear your voice too. But since we just talked a few days ago, I'm thinking you calling doesn't just have to do with hearing my voice. Did you get into it with Corbin? I tried to tell you to take it slow with him. He needs time to learn how to trust."

"It's not Corbin."

"Then what?" She hesitated. "Is it a girl?" There was a hopeful note in her voice. Shirlene had been hoping he'd meet a girl for the last thirteen years.

He heaved a long sigh. "Yes."

"It's a girl!" Shirlene said in a voice that wasn't even close to a whisper.

"Great," Billy said. "Now tell him to call back when it isn't two o'clock in the friggin' morning."

"Oh, hush up," Shirlene said before she returned to Jesse. "So tell me all about her, honey."

Jesse had never told Shirlene about the women he dated. Not only because he didn't want her getting the wrong idea, but also because they hadn't exactly been the type of women you brought home to Mama.

Not so with Liberty.

Once he started talking about her, he couldn't

seem to stop. He told Shirlene about her showing up at Cooper Springs and not being the least bit afraid of him. He told her about all their challenges—minus the seduction one—and how Liberty bested him most of the time. He told her about Liberty's business and what a great businesswoman she was. He went on and on and on until he finally realized he was babbling and cut off.

"Sorry. I guess I got carried away."

There was a distinct smile in Shirlene's voice when she spoke. "That's okay, baby. I'm a bit of a babbler too when I get excited about something. And it sounds like you're excited about Liberty. I can understand why. She sounds like a lovely girl . . . and a lot like you."

"That's the problem."

"What do you mean?"

"I don't think she's looking to get into a relationship. I'm not even sure I am."

"Then why do you sound so upset?"

It was a good question. "I don't know. We just had . . . this moment tonight. And after . . . well, I got scared and it ended badly and now I feel—"

"Like you lost something you didn't want to lose?"

He ran a hand through his hair and sighed. "Yeah."

"Oh, Jesse, my sweet baby boy," Shirlene said. "Showing your emotions has always come so hard for you. I get it. You've had a lot of heartache in your life and you'd just as soon not have any more. I think that's why you don't stick around in one place long enough to make close friends and have worked so hard to make Corbin love you. You don't want to feel rejected again like when . . ." She let the sentence trail off.

He finished it for her. "My mama and daddy rejected me."

"They didn't reject you, Jesse. They just don't know how to love. But you do. You have the biggest heart I've ever seen. You've opened it up to me and Billy and Adeline and Brody and Mia. To Corbin and I'm sure Sunny when she finally comes home. Now it's time to open it up all the way. I don't know what happened tonight between you and Liberty, but I'm sure you're not blameless. Men do stupid things when they have feelings for someone. Billy can tell you all about that."

"Hey now, sugar buns," Billy said. "I thought I've made up for my stupidity."

"It's an ongoing process . . . Bubba." When Shirlene used Billy's nickname, he usually shut up and conceded the argument. "Now you need to find that girl and tell her how you feel, Jesse."

"What if I don't know how I feel?"

"I think you know how you feel. You wouldn't have called me if you don't have strong feelings for this girl."

That was putting it mildly. His feelings for Liberty weren't just strong. They were overpowering. Which brought him to his main concern. "I don't want to get hurt, Mama. Or hurt her." He could almost see the tears welling in Shirlene's green eyes. She always cried when he called her *Mama*.

"Then take things slow, baby. Tell her that you really like her and you want to spend more time with her. Start there and see how things go."

"And if they go somewhere I'm not sure I want to go?"

"You worry about that when you get there. One step at a time, my sweet boy—Billy, stop that. I thought you were tired."

"I'm awake now."

Jesse rolled his eyes. Billy had never been able to keep his hands off Shirlene. He loved her with a passion that all the women in Bramble envied. Jesse wished he could love like that too. But Billy's blood didn't run through his veins. His cheating daddy's did.

"I'll let y'all go," he said. "Thank you, Shirl."

"You don't have to thank me, honey. That's what mamas are for. Here, Billy wants to talk to you."

Jesse figured he was going to get yelled at for calling so late. Instead, Billy surprised him. "Trust your heart, son. It will never steer you wrong. And even if you're not wrong, say you are. Believe me, it just makes life easier."

After Jesse hung up, he stood there in the parking lot for a long moment. Was Shirlene right? Should he tell Liberty how he felt and take it one step at a time? But what if she didn't feel the same way? Maybe she *had* just viewed tonight as a one-night stand. But even if she hadn't, she wouldn't let Jesse know. Like him, she didn't show her feelings easily. Especially her hurt. And having the person you just had sex with jump up like a scalded cat and race off to the bathroom without a word would be hurtful to anyone.

"Shit." He jumped in his truck and peeled out of the parking lot. With no traffic on the highway, it didn't take him long to get to the Holiday Ranch. Liberty's car was parked in front and the house was completely dark when he got there. He should turn right around and come back at a decent hour.

He couldn't. He needed to talk to Liberty and he needed to talk to her tonight. If he had to wake up the entire house, so be it. He just hoped her daddy didn't shoot first and ask questions later.

But it turned out Jesse didn't have to wake Hank Holiday. Before he could even knock on the door, Liberty stopped him.

"Just what the hell are you doing, Jesse Cates?"

He glanced over to see her sitting on the porch swing. She'd taken her boots off and her bare feet were resting on the edge of the swing, her arms wrapped around her legs as if she'd been giving them a hug. Her hair spilled around her like a moonlit waterfall. Once again, he found himself tongue tied with emotions.

"Hey."

She released her legs and set her feet on the floor. "Answer the question. What are you doing here?"

He took a few steps closer. Her face was in shadow, but he could see the tensing of her body. "I'm here to apologize for being an insensitive idiot."

"Like I told you, I don't need an apology. I can handle a one-night stand."

He hesitated for only a moment before he spoke. "Well, it seems that I can't. At least, not a one-night stand with you."

"And what does that mean?"

He sighed and ran a hand through his hair. "I don't know. I don't know what these feelings are I have for you, Libby. And that's what's making me so freaked out. You aren't like any woman I've ever met. You challenge me and you make me laugh . . . and you drive me completely crazy."

"So you came here to tell me that I drive you crazy?"

"Yes . . . no! Shit. I'm really messing this up. And that's the crux of the problem. I'm usually this calm, collected man who has no problems figuring things out. But I can't figure this"—he waved a hand between them—"out. All I know is that I want to be with you. Not because of a bet, but just because I like being with you. Which scares me shitless because I've never done this relationship stuff before. And I don't even know if I can."

"So you're saying you want to have a relationship with me, but you aren't sure you can have a relationship?"

Laid out like that, it sounded absolutely ridiculous. "You're right. I'm an idiot. Who would want to get involved with someone who is as emotionally screwed up as I am?" He turned, but she jumped up from the swing.

"Is that a challenge, Jesse Cates?"

He turned back to her. "No challenge, Lib. The stakes are too high."

"Shouldn't the one taking the challenge be the one who decides if the stakes are too high?" She stepped out of the shadow of the porch and into the moonlight. Moonlight that reflected off the tear tracks glistening on her cheeks.

His heart squeezed. "Libby? You've been crying."

She snorted. "Crying? Absolutely not. I was just cutting an onion. Like I said before, I'm not the type of woman who gets all weepy over a one-night stand."

He moved closer and gently traced the tear tracks with his finger. "It wasn't a one-night stand, Libby Lou. I think we both know that. But I don't want to hurt you and I'm afraid I will."

She hooked her arms around his shoulders. Her fingers sliding into the hair on the nape of his neck and causing need to pool in his gut. "You are so arrogant, Jesse Cates. Maybe I'll hurt you."

He was sure she would, but he couldn't stop himself from taking the chance.

Chapter Fifteen

"A WHOREHOUSE? I BOUGHT a whorehouse?"

Liberty looked away from the dilapidated mansion to the man sitting right next to her in the big ol' monster truck. Jesse had a stunned expression on his face. Since he was rarely stunned—by anything—she couldn't help laughing.

"You mean to tell me that Jesse Cates, a savvy businessman who never makes a decision without getting all the information, didn't know he bought one of the most infamous whorehouses in Texas?"

He continued to stare at the house they were parked in front of. "Not a clue. Although that explains why Mrs. Stokes was grinning like a cat that ate a canary the entire time we signed the paperwork." He glanced at her. "A whorehouse?"

"At one time, Mrs. Fields's rivaled The Chicken Ranch. Cowboys, civil war soldiers, oilmen, and senators flocked to Fanny's, who happens to be my great-great-great-great aunt on my mama's side. Her brother, who, ironically, was the town preacher and eventually responsible for closing the house down, was my great-great-great grandfather."

A big grin spread across his face. "I knew you had naughty blood running through your veins. Especially after last night."

Just the mention of the night before had her feeling all flushed and hot. Damned if Jesse didn't know it. His smile got even bigger as he leaned over and whispered in her ear.

"I didn't realize you were into bondage and pain—my bondage and pain. And I gotta tell you, darlin', we might need a safe word. My butt cheeks are still stinging."

She blinked. "Really?"

He sent her a wounded look. "Now would I lie about that? In fact, I think you need to kiss them and make them feel better."

She swatted his arm. "You are the orneriest man I know, Jesse Cates. Your mama should have blistered your butt."

"Believe me, honey, she did. Not just with her hand, but with a belt and a wooden spoon and a hanger. Whatever was handy." He had a teasing twinkle in his eyes, but there was something else too. Something that made her instantly concerned.

"No joking, Jesse. Your mama abused you?"

He shrugged. "She wasn't what you would call a loving mama."

Liberty's heart broke. "Oh, Jesse. I didn't know. If I had, I never would have spanked you last night. I'm so sorry. It must have been traumatic for you."

"Hey, now." He cradled her face in his hands. "Believe me, the sweet spanking you gave me last night was about as far from traumatic as a spanking can get."

Which meant that the other spankings he'd gotten *had* been traumatic. The mere thought of her ornery little redheaded Opie Wolverine being abused made her want to weep.

It also made her madder than a hornet.

"Does your mama still live in Houston?"

"Yes. Why?"

"No reason. I was just wondering."

He studied her for a long moment before a big grin spread over his face. "Are you going to go hunt her down and kick her ass, darlin'?"

She scowled. "I'm definitely thinking about it."

He laughed before he leaned in and softly kissed her. "Thank you, but I think it's best if we leave the past in the past." He gave her another kiss, this one longer and deeper. "For now, I'd rather concentrate on the present." He looked back at the house and a look of awe filled his face. "I own a whorehouse." He opened the truck door. "Come on! Just wait until you see inside."

Liberty had been inside of Fanny Fields's house before. Growing up, it had been a rite of passage to break into the mansion at night and see how long you could stay without getting scared. Liberty had stayed the least amount of time. She had always been scared of the supernatural and the old, crumbling house was the perfect place for ghosts to live.

It still looked that way.

Once inside, they had to step over piles of water-damaged ceiling plaster to get to the rest of the house. But Jesse didn't seem to be bothered by the mess, or the falling-down ceilings, or the holes rodents had made in the walls.

"Would you look at this bannister and stairs? That's solid maple, darlin'. And do you see the craftsmanship? They don't make staircases like that anymore. Just wait until you see the bedrooms."

The upstairs wasn't quite as bad as the downstairs, but it still wasn't good. Most of the windows were broken out and wind whistled through them, blowing the threadbare curtains and making them look like tattered ghosts.

"You have lost your mind, Jesse Cates," she said as they headed back downstairs so he could show her the carriage house. "There's no money to make from this old house."

"I don't know about that. The more I hear about this house, the more I think it's worth saving."

"For what?"

He shrugged. "I don't know. Maybe I just want to see it returned to its former beauty." He squeezed her hand and winked at her. "I happen to like beautiful things."

Liberty shouldn't get all mushy inside over a compliment from a natural-born charmer. Jesse had no doubt used his lines on numerous women. But knowing that didn't stop her from melting.

She had been doing a lot of melting lately.

She melted when he smiled. She melted when

he laughed. She melted when he looked at her. And she really melted when he touched her. She wished she could stop the melting, but the only way to stop it was to let him go. She couldn't do that. At least, not yet. She was enjoying their time together too much.

For the last five days, since they had decided to give this thing between them a chance, Jesse had arrived at the ranch bright and early ... with Tay-Tay in tow. Inside of devoting his attention to her, he devoted his attention to her family. He'd helped Hank clean out the chicken coop and Mimi pull weeds and Darla clean rugs. He'd brought muffins for breakfast and steaks for dinner and Mimi a rosebush.

But regardless of how much time he spent with her family, he always found time to take her somewhere fun: drives through the countryside looking at the last of the spring flowers, horseback riding at the Remington Ranch, and picnics at Cooper Springs.

At night, they'd go back to Corbin's trailer where Jesse would fulfill every fantasy she'd ever had ... and some she'd never had but now did.

Jesse *was* a charmer. He had certainly charmed her.

"So what do you think?" he asked once he had finished showing her the carriage house. A building just as dilapidated as the house.

"I think a stiff wind could knock it over."

"You have absolutely no vision, Libby Lou." He waved a hand. "This is a gold mine just waiting to be mined. All it needs is a little love and money."

"And a bulldozer."

Her cellphone rang. As soon as she saw it was Belle, Liberty figured it had to do with the Holiday Sisters Events' calendar Liberty had just filled in that morning. She knew her sister would be upset. Liberty was pretty mad at herself for taking on all the town's events.

"I need to get this," she said.

Jesse gave her a brief kiss. "Take your time, darlin'. I want to check out the antique furniture Mrs. Stokes said was in the attic of the carriage house."

Liberty waited until he walked away before she answered the phone. "Hey, Belly. I guess you saw the new events I put on the calendar."

"What in the world were you thinking telling all those folks in Wilder we'd do their events, Libby? Especially when some are scheduled in July and August and neither one of us will be there then. You're heading back to Houston in a week and I'm not planning on staying past June. Not even that long if Jesse can convince Corbin to sell the ranch to Rome. Has he talked with him yet?"

"Jesse wants to talk to Corbin in person and he's due back any day now. So don't worry, Belly. Jesse gave me his word he'll handle it and he will. As for the added events to the calendar, I know I shouldn't have agreed to help, but they're our people, Belle. I couldn't say no. We can do most of the planning from Houston. On the weekend of the events, I don't mind coming home."

There was a long pause before Belle spoke.

"What happened to the woman who was ticked off she had to spend any time in Wilder?"

"I guess she realized that home isn't such a bad place to be." Especially if Jesse was there.

Although she knew he wouldn't be there for long. He was a drifter. He made no bones about it. He acted like he was interested in renovating Mrs. Fields', but she knew it was just something to keep his business mind occupied while he was waiting for Corbin to return. And maybe that was what she was as well. Just someone to pass the time with while he waited for Corbin.

Not wanting to even consider the possibility, she changed the subject. "So have you found any office space to rent?"

"Unfortunately, no. The places we can afford are no bigger than what we have now. The places that are bigger, we can't afford. It looks like my plan wasn't such a good one after all. I've always been bad at making decisions."

"That's not true, Belly. Buying our own tables and chairs will pay off in the long run. So will having a bigger space. We just need to keep looking for a place that will hold all our event supplies and be cheap enough we can—"

She cut off as she stared at the carriage house. It had been built to store multiple carriages. It had four large sliding wood doors and plenty of space inside for horses and carriages . . . and decorations and tables and chairs.

A brush of lips on her neck had her releasing a startled squeak.

"What happened?" Belle asked.

Liberty closed her eyes as Jesse kissed his way along her neck. "Nothing, Belly. I thought I saw a mouse. I'll call you back later."

"A mouse?" Jesse whispered in her ear as soon as she hung up. He took her hand and placed it on his fly. The feel of his stiff erection made her knees weak. "Does this feel like a mouse to you, darlin'?" He nipped at her neck. "Have you ever made love in a whorehouse, Libby Lou?"

His choice of words had more than her knees melting. He had never used the term "making love" before and it did something to her heart.

Her voice trembled with need. "N-N-No."

"You want to?"

At the moment, she couldn't think of anything she wanted more. Only one thing stopped her. "I refuse to do it on an old whorehouse mattress."

He chuckled against her skin. "Which is why I bought a brand-new mattress for the big ol' brass bed in the corner bedroom."

He'd also bought new sheets. On those sheets, he used his talented fingers and lips to make her scream his name over and over. Much later, when Liberty was completely sated and cuddled against Jesse's hard naked chest, her mind returned to the carriage house.

"How big is the attic over the carriage house? Is it big enough for an office and maybe a conference room?"

Jesse stopped drawing circles on her arm. "More than big enough. Why?"

She sat up. "You know how I told you that Belle and I were looking for bigger office space in Houston. Well, Belle hasn't been able to find anything that is bigger than what we have and fits our budget." She hesitated. "But what about if we rented the carriage house from you."

Jesse blinked. "You mean move your company from Houston and relocate here?"

She sighed. "You're right. That's crazy."

He sat up. "I don't know about that. The carriage house is the size of a warehouse and would be plenty big enough to store everything event planners would need and then some."

"But most of our customers live in Houston."

He cocked an eyebrow. "From all the events you have lined up for the townsfolk, it sounds like there are a lot of people right here who need your services. And you said your family's barn is a gold mine as far as a venue goes and you think people wouldn't mind traveling here from Houston for weddings. So if they wouldn't mind traveling from Houston, they wouldn't mind traveling from Austin. Which is close to the same distance."

He was right. They could double their clients. Excitement started to tingle in her stomach, but it died quickly. "It's a falling-down mess."

"And that's fixable. When is your lease up on your office space?"

"In a couple months."

"That's plenty of time to get the carriage house finished."

"But we can't pay for the renovations."

"It's my building. I'm the one who will pay for it to get renovated. You'll pay rent to me." He smiled wickedly. "In fact, I'll enjoy making you pay."

She didn't laugh at his teasing. This was business and she never joked about business. "We'd have to have a contract."

He sobered. "Of course."

"And I'm not paying you a pretty penny. This is Wilder, after all."

The grin came back. "I'm sure we can come up with a contract that meets both our needs."

She stared at him as she finally realized what moving her business here would mean. "Belle and I would have to move back here."

His eyes softened. "I don't see that being a problem. You might act like a hardnosed city girl, Libby Lou, but it's quite obvious that being here makes you happy. This is where you can be your true self."

"And exactly what is my true self?"

He reached out and yanked on one of her braids. "A sweet little braid-wearin', roll-bakin', skinny-dippin' country gal."

She lifted her eyebrows. "Sweet?"

He laughed. "Okay, maybe not sweet. But sweet is overrated as far as I'm concerned. I prefer my country gals to be full of sass and vinegar." He went to kiss her, but she placed a hand on his chest.

"Do you really think we could move the business here and it would still be successful?"

"With you at the helm, I don't see how it can fail."

It was crazy. She knew it was crazy. But the

more she thought about it, the more excited she became. She got out of bed and started to pace.

"You're right. Wilder is centrally located. Although it's still over an hour away from Houston and Austin—more if the city traffic is bad. And while some people won't mind as long as they can have an authentic barn wedding, the drive might deter other people. I just wish there was a hotel close, at least for the wedding party. A cute boutique hotel . . . or better yet, a sweet little bed-and—"

She cut off and glanced around the room as a thought struck her.

"Fanny Fields' Bed and Breakfast," she breathed. "It would be perfect. People could have their weddings in an old country barn and their honeymoons in an infamous house of ill repute. What couple wouldn't jump at the chance to do that? We could research what the rooms looked like online and try to replicate them." She snapped her fingers and pointed at Jesse. "There's this antique dealer in Houston. I did a wedding for her daughter and I'm sure she would be willing to do the research and track down what we need if we bought most of the furniture through her. Mama said that Fanny named all the rooms after desserts she loved to eat? Bananas Foster. Strawberry Shortcake. Chocolate Truffle. We could keep those names and maybe use them as a theme for each room. We could even get Sheryl Ann to bake us some signature muffins to serve every morning with cute but naughty names. People would eat it up."

She glanced at Jesse to find him staring at her with something that looked like panic. With a sinking stomach, she realized what she'd done. Jesse had made it clear he wanted to take their relationship one day at a time. And suddenly, she had jumped from renting the carriage house to renovating and running a bed-and-breakfast in Wilder . . . together.

What had she been thinking? She didn't want to run a business with Jesse. And a bed-and-breakfast? Where had that come from? She might follow a few bed-and-breakfast sites online because she enjoyed looking at their quaint, homey décor and comfy, inviting rooms and country breakfast buffets all set up on an antique sideboard with crocks of homemade butter and jam, but she didn't want to own one.

She had a business.

A business in Houston.

She forced a laugh. "I'm sorry. My brain sometimes gets the best of me. Of course you don't want to run a bed-and-breakfast here in Wilder. And I don't either. I was just rambling to ramble. Turning this falling-down house into a bed-and-breakfast is a crazy idea. Even turning the carriage house into our event-planning business doesn't make sense. Holiday Sisters Events belongs in Houston. And so do I."

"I don't agree," he said. "You belong here, Libby."

And where do you belong, Jesse?

The question popped into her head, but she didn't ask it. Instead, she started gathering her clothes. "I better get home. I promised Mimi I would help her pick cherries."

They didn't talk much on the drive home. Jesse seemed to be in deep thought and Liberty knew she had sent him into panic mode. She wouldn't be surprised if after he dropped her off, she never heard from him again.

The thought sent a sharp pang of pain through her heart. She realized that, regardless of how much she tried to tell herself this was just a brief fling, she had started to fall for Jesse. She had let her guard down and gotten too attached to a man with commitment issues. After finding out about his mother, she now understood his fear of relationships. Unfortunately, that knowledge wasn't going to make the pain any less when he did leave.

And he would.

His reaction today proved it.

Decker's sheriff's car and Rome's truck were parked in front when Jesse and Liberty arrived at the ranch. Sweetie, Decker, Rome, Cloe, Mama, Daddy, and Mimi were all gathered on the front porch. Liberty hadn't known her sisters and brothers-in-law were coming over for supper and the sight of them lifted her depressed spirits.

"Hey, y'all!" she said as Jesse helped her down from the truck. Her smile faded when she saw their somber faces. "What's wrong?"

"I'll tell you what's wrong." Hank glanced at Jesse and waved the document he held in his hand. "We're being evicted!"

Chapter Sixteen

JESSE'S BRAIN WAS still trying to wrap around Liberty wanting to run a bed-and-breakfast together so it took him a second to comprehend what Hank Holiday had just said. When it finally sank in, he didn't wait to be invited up on the Holidays' porch. He took the steps two at a time and held out his hand to Hank.

"Could I take a look at that, sir?"

Once Hank handed it to him, Jesse quickly scanned the document. It was exactly what Hank said it was. An eviction notice. If they weren't gone by July 1st, the county sheriff, who just happened to be Decker, would be there to escort them off the property.

"It came with this." Rome handed him the piece of paper he held. "It's the judge-signed foreclosure. Your friend must know someone high up to get it pushed through all the usual red tape so quickly."

Corbin knew a lot of people who had connections—Jesse had made sure of it. He'd introduced Corbin to anyone he thought could help his brother's business succeed. He hadn't thought

Corbin would use those connections to throw someone out of their home. The Corbin he knew wouldn't. Something wasn't adding up.

He glanced through the document before he handed it back to Rome. "I need to talk to Corbin and get this straightened out." He glanced at Mimi, who looked pale and lost. "I promise you I will, Ms. Mimi. Even if I have to fly to Paris myself."

"He's not in Paris," Decker said. "I saw him in town on my way out here."

Jesse was surprised Corbin hadn't texted or called him to tell him he was in town, but he tried not to show it. "Then we should have this all figured out by tonight."

Hank snorted. "I'll believe it when I hear it straight from the horse's mouth. Or more like the jackass's mouth."

"Hank!" Darla scolded. "If Jesse says he's going to get it worked out, I believe him." She smiled at him. "Thank you, Jesse. We appreciate you helping us."

"Well, don't just stand there, boy," Mimi said. "Go talk to Corbin. When you two get things figured out, you both come on back here for supper and we'll celebrate. You haven't tried my homemade elderberry wine yet and I think it's time to crack open some bottles."

"Thank you for the invite, Ms. Mimi, but Corbin might be a little jet lagged." Jesse looked at Liberty. "But I'll be back."

Liberty followed him out to his truck and voiced the same question he had been asking himself. "Why didn't Corbin call to tell you he was back?"

"I don't know. But I guess I'll find out shortly." He started to climb into his truck, but then stopped and turned to her. "Look, Libby, about the way I acted earlier. Your bed-and-breakfast idea just took me a little by surprise, is all."

"You don't have to explain." She shook her head. "It was a silly idea."

"It's not silly. It's just that I never really thought about being—"

She cut him off. "I get it. Why would a successful businessman want to run a bed-and-breakfast in a Podunk town?" She tapped the brim of his hat. "Now go save my family's ranch."

He started to get in his truck, but once again stopped. He knew her family was watching, but he didn't care. He swept her into his arms and kissed her. He planned to just give her a quick kiss, but as soon as her lips melted against his, he was lost. When he finally drew back and looked into those pretty green eyes, a feeling washed over him. A feeling that pushed him to say something he had no business saying.

So instead, he just smiled. "See you soon, Libby Lou."

Once he got to the trailer, he found a brand-new white dually pickup truck with the dealer tag still on it parked out front. It looked like Corbin had traded his Cadillac SUV in for a truck almost as big as Jesse's. Jesse grinned as he parked and hopped out.

He thought he'd find Corbin sleeping off his

jet lag. He should have known better. Like him, Corbin didn't sleep. Instead, he was sitting at the scarred kitchen table working on his laptop with Tay-Tay curled in his lap.

He and Jesse looked nothing alike. Jesse looked like their daddy while Corbin had taken after his blond-haired, blue-eyed mama. Those blue eyes lit up when Jesse stepped into the trailer.

"Hey, Jess!"

Jesse was just as happy to see his brother. "Hey, yourself. I see you had a little truck envy." He glanced out the window. "But yours still isn't as big as mine."

Corbin laughed. "Yeah, but it's newer and doesn't need a jump start every time it gets cold."

"Hey, Bubba's truck will outrun yours any day—or maybe not outrun yours, but run over yours." He walked over and slapped Corbin on the back. "Good to see you, little bro. Why didn't you text me to tell me you were back?"

"I wanted to surprise you." Corbin grinned. "Or not me as much as—" Before he could finish, Tay-Tay woke up from her nap. Surprisingly, she didn't hiss. In fact, she stood up on Corbin's lap and greeted Jesse with a soft meow. When he petted her head, she pushed into his hand.

Corbin grinned. "I see you and Tay made up."

"I still get the occasional scratch, but we've formed a truce ... with the help of Mimi the cat whisperer."

Corbin's smile faded. "Mimi? Mimi Holiday?"

Jesse pulled the other chair out from the table and sat down. "We need to talk, Whitty."

"Obviously. Since when are you on a first-name basis with the Holidays' grandma?"

"Since I got to know her and the rest of the Holidays. What are you thinking foreclosing on their ranch?"

Corbin cocked his head. "What am I thinking? I'm thinking that I loaned them money in good faith and they broke the contract."

"But Rome is willing to pay off the loan. With interest."

Corbin shrugged. "I don't want the money. I want the ranch."

All Jesse could do was stare at him. "The ranch? Why would you want the ranch? Land prices are down."

"I'm not selling it. I'm living in it."

If he had said he wanted to be a pizza delivery guy, Jesse couldn't have been more surprised. "Living in it? Since when do you want to live on a ranch? You love your fancy apartment in Houston."

"It's not about me. Sunny needs a home."

Jesse knew Corbin adored his sister and wanted to give her everything, but he didn't get this. "But why a ranch? You know nothing about cattle and horses."

"Then I'll learn. You said yourself that I'm a fast study. I learned the loan business in just a year."

It was the truth. Corbin had taken to business like a duck to water. Just like Jesse, he had a natural ability to make money. Which was why Jesse had pushed him to start his own business. And he had never interfered with Corbin's choices or decisions.

Until now.

"Okay. If you want a ranch for Sunny, I'll help you find one. Hell, I'll even invest in your cattle-raising business. Just not the Holiday Ranch. Let Rome pay off the loan, Corbin."

Corbin stared at him for a long moment before a knowing look entered his eyes. "They got to you, didn't they?"

"What?"

"The Holidays. They sucked you in just like they've sucked in everyone else in this town."

"They didn't suck me in. I just discovered they're good people is all."

Corbin set Tay-Tay on the floor and got up from the chair. "Good people? You think they're good people. Well, let me tell you about those good people, Jess. For five years our uncle busted his ass for the Holiday Ranch, and do you know how Hank thanked him? He fired him."

Jesse was more than a little surprised. Not about Hank firing their uncle, but about Liberty not mentioning it. And there was probably a good reason for that.

"Are you sure Hank fired him? Or is that Uncle Dan's version? Because I can't see Hank firing a man for no good reason. Especially one who worked for him for so long. I never met our uncle, but if he was anything like our daddy, he stretched the truth. If he didn't, I'm sure there was a good reason he got fired. You told me yourself he had a drinking problem like Daddy."

"Maybe he did have a drinking problem, but instead of firing him, Hank should have offered him help." Corbin hesitated. "They should have offered us all help."

Now they seemed to be getting to the root of Corbin's problem with the Holidays.

Jesse sighed. "I know it wasn't easy for you and Sunny being pawned off on one relative right after the other. But the Holidays aren't to blame. Our daddy and your mama are."

"I'm not blaming the Holidays for that." Corbin's face hardened. "But they could have made Sunny's life a little easier. You don't know her yet, but Sunny is just like her namesake. She's bright and full of life. It about killed me when she came home every day crying because she didn't have any friends and had to eat lunch by herself. And you know the friend she wanted most? Noelle Holiday. But Noelle already had her clique and she never gave Sunny the time of day." He paused and a hurt look entered his eyes. "And I knew how Sunny felt because I fell for my own Holiday."

Jesse knew what name Corbin was going to say before he said it.

"Liberty. Beautiful, dynamic, take-your-breath-away Liberty." Corbin smiled sardonically. "From the moment I saw her, I was a goner. I followed her around like a little lost puppy. I wrote her poems. I brought her flowers. Our senior year, when I finally got up enough nerve to ask her out and she said yes, I thought I had won the fuckin' lottery."

He laughed, but there was no humor in it. "You want to know what those good people did to me, Jesse? They pulled the twin switch. Instead of Liberty, I got Belle. All because Liberty had started going steady with the quarterback of another high school. Rather than just be honest, they thought I wouldn't notice the difference. But I noticed. I played along with their hurtful little game, but I knew. And I never forgot."

Jesse now understood why Corbin seemed to have a vendetta against the Holidays. Having been a kid with crappy parents, he knew how you envied the kids who had a big loving family who came to all their games and activities to cheer them on. Jesse had eventually gotten to be one of those kids. He *had* gotten the big loving family who came to all his school functions and activities and cheered him on.

Corbin hadn't.

All he'd had was the dream. The dream that included the same girl Jesse dreamed of. He didn't want to believe Liberty had talked Belle into the twin switch, but it sounded like something a teenage kid would do. Jesse had done plenty of dumb things as a teenager that he later regretted. Still, once again, he wondered why Liberty hadn't told him. Maybe she didn't think it had been a big deal.

"They were teenage girls, Corbin," he said. "Teenage girls do things like that. You can't hold that against them and punish them by taking their family's ranch."

"I'm not punishing them, Jess. I'm over what Liberty and Belle Holiday did to me."

"Then let Rome pay off the loan and buy another ranch."

"I don't want another ranch. I want the ranch Sunny dreamed about living on. Uncle Dan only took us out to the Holiday Ranch with him a few times before he was fired, but that was enough for Sunny to fall in love with it. Every picture she drew after that was of the house and the barn and the oak with the swing. I want her to have her dream."

Jesse stared at him. "At the cost of taking it away from the little old woman who had the same dream?"

Corbin shrugged. "The Holidays made their bed, Jesse. I didn't force Mimi to sign the contract."

As Jesse studied his brother, the truth dawned. "This was your plan all along, wasn't it? You knew the ranch was in financial trouble and you had Oleander Investments give Hank a way to consolidate all his loans, knowing he wouldn't be able to pay you back."

"Isn't that what you taught me, big brother? Figure out when the odds are in your favor and go in for the kill?"

That was exactly what Jesse had taught him. He sighed and ran a hand through his hair. "Damn it, Corbin. Why didn't you tell me?"

"Why would I? You've never cared how I run the business. Now suddenly you've fallen in love with the Holidays and want to put them before your own family."

That stung. And pissed him off. He got to his feet. "I'm not putting them before my own family. I'll buy you and Sunny a damn ranch that's just as nice, if not nicer. Just leave the Holidays' ranch alone!"

"What's going on?"

The question had Jesse turning to the door of the bedroom. A young woman stood there. He had seen pictures. But seeing pictures of his half sister and actually seeing her in person were two different things. While he and Corbin looked nothing alike, he and Sunny looked like paternal twins. Same strawberry-blond hair. Same freckles. Same soft brown eyes.

Eyes that lit up.

"Jesse?" She charged across the room and dove into his arms. "I always wanted another brother!"

Chapter Seventeen

ALL THROUGH SUPPER, Liberty watched the clock on the stove and listened for the rumbling sound of Jesse's truck. She knew the rest of her family was doing the same thing. Mama, Mimi, Daddy, Cloe, and Sweetie barely spoke as they ate the tater tot casserole Mama had made for supper. It was Decker and Rome who kept the conversation going.

"Ms. Peterson got a new Mini Cooper," Decker said as he watched Sweetie pick at her food with a concerned look. "Today was the third time in two weeks that I had to pull her over for speeding. I hated to give my favorite librarian a ticket, but I'd already given her two warnings. Still, Melba gave me a thorough scolding when I got back to the office about Ms. Peterson just needing to sow a little wild oats after her husband left her."

"You're lucky Melba just gave you a scolding, instead of one of her foster pets. She came by today with a pudgy pug that she tried to pawn off on us." Rome dished up some more casserole. But instead of putting it on his plate, he put it on Cloe's. "Remember you're eating for two, honey."

Cloe shook her head. "Thank you, but I'm just not hungry."

Liberty wasn't hungry either. She was scared, but she couldn't help trying to calm her family's fears. "Jesse is going to get everything figured out. He's probably on his way back here to tell us the good news as I speak."

But when they'd finished eating and all the dishes were cleaned and put away, Daddy had had enough waiting around. He grabbed his hat off the rack by the door. "I'm heading to Corbin's to see what the hell is going on."

"No, Daddy," Sweetie said. "We need to give Jesse more time."

"I agree," Mama said. "Maybe they went to the Hellhole and just lost track of the time. How many times have you been late for, or completely missed, supper, Hank, because you ran into a friend at Bobby's? Jesse hasn't seen his friend for a while. I'm sure they have a lot to catch up on."

"I'm sure that's it," Cloe agreed. "Jesse just hasn't been able to get away. If he doesn't make it tonight, I'm sure he'll be here bright and early in the morning." She got up from the couch. "We better get going, Rome."

Sweetie stood. "We need to get home too."

Everyone walked out to the porch to say goodbye. Once her sisters and their husbands had driven away, her parents went inside, leaving Liberty and Mimi on the porch. Feeling the need to ease her grandmother's fears, Liberty spoke,

"Jesse won't give up, Mimi. He's one of the

best negotiators I've ever met at getting what he wants."

Mimi sat down on the swing and patted the spot next to her. When Liberty was seated, Mimi studied her with intent eyes. "I don't doubt for a second that Jesse will do his best." She hesitated. "And not because he likes your mama's apple pies. After that kiss he gave you earlier, I figure I know what Jesse wants."

Liberty didn't deny it. She knew Jesse wanted her. Just not enough to stay.

"Don't be thinking you hear wedding bells, Mimi. Jesse's not the marrying kind."

Mimi's eyebrow lifted. "You usually say that you're not the marrying kind. Are you starting to change your mind about marriage being the worst thing that could happen to an independent, strong woman? Does Jesse have you starting to doubt your belief that marriage takes your independence?"

She shrugged. "It doesn't seem to have taken Cloe's and Sweetie's. So I guess it all depends on the man."

Mimi pushed the swing and sent it swaying. "And is Jesse the kind of man who will let his wife be who she is?"

Liberty thought over the question. There was no doubt in her mind Jesse would allow the woman he married to be who she was. He wouldn't try to change her or suffocate her. In fact, he seemed to love challenging Liberty to be even stronger and more independent. It was too bad he wasn't the marrying kind. Even if he was, she wasn't.

And not just because she was scared about losing her independence.

"I can't have kids, Mimi."

Mimi didn't even flinch or act the least bit surprised. Of course, she had witnessed Liberty's horrible periods and emergency room visits when she was a teenager. "And what does that have to do with getting married?"

"Men, even men who say they don't want children, don't want the option taken from them. I don't want to be the woman they end up resenting."

"And you think Jesse will be the type of man to resent his wife for something she can't help?"

She didn't know why tears sprang to her eyes, but there they were. "No, but he doesn't want to marry me, Mimi. He's made no bones about struggling with relationships."

Mimi snorted. "Everyone struggles with relationships. If they say they don't, they're lying. The question is 'Does he think you're worth the struggle?'"

She brushed a tear from her cheek. "I don't know. But if he doesn't, you don't need to worry. I'll survive."

Mimi placed an arm around her shoulders and pulled her close. "Of course you will. Of all my granddaughters, you are a survivor, Liberty Lou Holiday, and I don't doubt for a second that you can survive without Jesse or any man." She paused. "But there's a difference between simply surviving and living life to the fullest. If Jesse is the kind of man who lets you be the strong, independent woman you are, why would you want to survive without him?"

"I don't think Jesse is going to give me that choice."

"But if he did? If he showed up here tonight and said, 'Libby Lou, you're the woman of my dreams and I can't live without you,' what would you say?"

The answer came immediately. She just couldn't bring herself to say it.

But Mimi knew. Her grandmother had always been good at reading her.

"So I guess you have a choice, Libby Lou. You can sit here hoping your Prince Charming shows up and says those words . . . or you can take matters in your own hands and go after what you want." She gave her a tight hug before she got up from the swing. When she glanced down at Liberty, there was a twinkle in her eyes. "I know my strong, independent granddaughter will make the right choice."

After Mimi left, Liberty sat there on the swing thinking about everything her grandmother had said. Mimi was right. All her life, Liberty had worked hard to prove to herself, her family, and everyone else that she was a strong, independent woman who could do quite nicely without a man. But being strong and independent didn't mean she had to be alone for the rest of her life. Some people didn't take away your strength and independence. Some people only added to it.

Jesse had forced her out of her one-track mind

and made her notice the world around her. He made her laugh and cry and feel things she'd never felt before. He challenged her to enjoy life. To see more. To feel more. To be more.

She was more with Jesse. So much more.

So why would she let him go?

She jumped up and hurried into the house. Daddy and Mama looked surprised when she grabbed her purse and keys. Mimi only smiled.

"I'm going to see Jesse," she said. "Don't wait up."

On the way to Corbin's trailer, she went well over the speed limit. She wasn't in a hurry to find out about the ranch. She was in a hurry to see Jesse and tell him she thought their relationship was worth fighting for. Correction, she knew it was worth fighting for.

When she got to Corbin's, Jesse's truck and another white truck were parked in the yard so she parked just outside the rusty chicken-wire fence. As she headed toward the front door, she could hear laughter coming from the trailer. It looked like Mama had been right and Jesse and Corbin were so busy catching up that they *had* lost track of the time. She took the laughter as a good sign that everything had gone well with Corbin.

But she wasn't concerned about the ranch now. All she was concerned about was Jesse feeling the same way she did. She thought he did. But what if she couldn't convince him that what they had was special enough to give a chance?

Her hand shook as she knocked on the door.

The laughter inside faded and a few seconds later the door swung open.

It took her a moment to recognize Corbin. In high school, he had been a tall, skinny kid with shaggy, unkempt hair and acne. Now he was an even taller, muscular man with styled hair that swept back from a handsome face with a smooth complexion. As soon as he saw her, the smile he had on his face turned to a scowl.

"Well, if it isn't Liberty Holiday. Or are you Belle? I always struggle to tell the difference." There was a sarcastic tone to his voice that made Liberty more than a little leery.

"Hey, Corbin. How have you been?"

Before he could answer, a woman moved next to Corbin. Jesse stepped up behind her. The similarity in his and the woman's features was startling.

"Libby?" Jesse said.

She pinned on a smile. "Sorry to interrupt. I just wanted to talk to you, but we can talk later." She looked at the woman. "I didn't realize you had family in town." She held out a hand. "Liberty Holiday."

The woman took her hand and smiled brightly. "We've already met. I'm Sunny Whitlock, Corbin's sister." She glanced over her shoulder at Jesse. "And Jesse's."

Her words completely blindsided Liberty. "You're Jesse's sister?" She glanced at Jesse. "I don't understand."

"Of course you don't," Corbin said. "Your parents didn't switch partners like ours . . . but you and your sister didn't mind switching boyfriends."

Liberty was so stunned about Jesse being related to Corbin and Sunny, she didn't even try to grasp what Corbin was talking about.

"That's enough, Whitty." Jesse stepped out the door and closed it behind him. He took her arm and led her down the rickety steps. Still stunned, she allowed it. But once they were at the bottom, the truth finally sunk in and she jerked away from his grasp and whirled on him.

"You're Corbin's brother!"

He held out his hands. "Calm down, Libby."

"Calm down? Calm down? Like hell I'm going to calm down. Answer the question. Are you or are you not, Sunny and Corbin's brother?"

He sighed. "Half brother. We have the same father."

She felt like she had the time she'd been tossed off a horse and had all the wind knocked out of her. She had trusted Jesse. She had completely trusted him. And he'd been lying to her all along. Her voice shook with anger and hurt.

"So you're not friends. You're family. Not once when you were telling me about your adoptive family did you mention Sunny and Corbin."

"Because I didn't find out about them until a couple years ago. That's when we went into business together."

"You're business partners? What business?" When Jesse didn't say anything, she knew. Once again, she felt the searing pain of betrayal. "So it's not just Corbin foreclosing on my family's ranch. It's you too."

He shook his head. "No. I didn't have anything

to do with your family's loan. But I still should have told you that Corbin was my brother and business partner. At first, I didn't because I didn't think you needed to know. Later, it was because . . ." He let the sentence drift off, but Liberty didn't need him to finish it.

"You wanted to get me into bed."

"That's not it at all, Libby." He went to reach for her, but she stepped back.

"Oh, come on, Jesse. There's no need to lie anymore. That was the bet, wasn't it? And you won. You got me in bed. Not just for one night, but for many." She forced a laugh. "Damn, you are good at getting the most out of a deal."

"Stop it, Libby. It wasn't like that and you know it."

"Then what was it, Jesse? Was it love?" Even in the darkness, she could read the panicked look on his face. A dagger sliced her heart and she struggled to keep her voice from trembling. "Of course it wasn't. It was just a little fun while you waited for your brother to get back." A thought struck her. "You never planned to talk to him about the eviction notice, did you? I bet you never even planned to talk him out of foreclosing on the ranch." Her temper flared and she swung at him. "You bastard!"

He easily caught her wrist. "Stop it, Liberty. You're letting your temper keep you from thinking logically."

"Don't tell me I'm not thinking logically. I know exactly how you think, Jesse Cates. You said yourself that you and I are two peas in a pod.

My family will always come first with me. Then business. Everything else comes after that. Which means the deal you made with a woman you had a spring fling with is third on your list."

"A spring fling? So now we went from a one-night stand to a spring fling?" He snorted. "Wow, Libby Lou, I'm honored."

She jerked away from him. "Please don't act like you thought it was more. You're too terrified to make any kind of commitment and we both know it."

"And you're not? How many men have you been in a serious relationship with? Just one name."

"At least I can commit to something. You can't even commit to a place to live." She used her hands to bracket a headline. 'Jesse Cates, Billionaire World Traveler!'" She lowered her hands. "More like 'Jesse Cates, Lying Loser.'"

Even in the dark, she could see the anger flare in his eyes. "Let's talk about lying, shall we? Why didn't you tell me about what you did to Corbin?"

"What I did to Corbin? It was a high school crush. Nothing ever happened between us."

"I wouldn't say agreeing to a date and then sending your sister in your stead is nothing."

Her eyes widened. "I never sent Belle in my stead."

"That's not what Corbin told me. He said Belle pretended like she was you."

"Belly wouldn't do that. Corbin must be confused. All I asked her to do was tell him that I was sick."

"Were you sick?"

"No, but what difference does that make?" She stared at him as the truth dawned. "That's why he's taking the ranch? He's pissed at me because I pretended to be sick and went out with another guy? I was all of seventeen, for God's sake." She turned for the door. "I'll be happy to apologize if that's what it takes."

Jesse caught her arm. "He doesn't want an apology. He wants the ranch."

She looked back at him. "But why?"

He sighed. "Because he wants to give Sunny the home she never had."

"Then let him choose another home. I'm sure the Cates family has enough money to buy him whatever he and Sunny want."

"He doesn't want another home. He wants the Holiday Ranch."

"So stop him. You're not only his business partner. You're his brother. Stop him."

A resigned look came over his face. "I can't."

"You can't or you won't?"

He stared back at her for a long moment before he spoke. "I won't."

She'd come there hoping to get Jesse to fight for her. To fight for them. With just two words, that hope had been crushed like his truck tires crushed sagebrush. She wanted to hate him, but she couldn't. She understood exactly what he was thinking. He was fighting for his family . . . just like she would fight for hers.

"Then I guess the battle lines have been drawn." She turned and walked away.

Chapter Eighteen

～

JESSE WOKE WITH one helluva hangover. It didn't help that there were no curtains and blinding sunlight burned his retinas as soon as he opened his eyes.

As he sat up and blinked the dismal room into focus, all the whiskey he'd consumed the night before sloshed around in his belly and he wished like hell he had gotten a hotel room with blackout curtains and a working bathroom . . . and maybe windows with actual glass panes. Or he should have just headed home to Bramble. Of course, he'd been too drunk to drive. Which was why he had ended up here. Stumbling down the street to Mrs. Fields's boardinghouse had been safer than getting behind the wheel. His truck was still parked at the Hellhole. He didn't relish the thought of walking down the street to get it.

But it was time to leave Wilder.

There was no reason for him to stay.

The thought had pain slicing through his chest, adding to the throbbing in his head and the rolling of his stomach. He jumped out of bed and barely made it to one of the paneless windows before he threw up. After he'd emptied his entire stomach on the overgrown bushes beneath the window, he felt better but still like death warmed over.

"I wanted to get to know you, but seeing my new brother's naked behind wasn't what I had in mind."

He straightened so quickly that he banged his head on the top of the windowpane. It felt like he'd been coldcocked with a two-by-four.

"Holy shit!" He grabbed his head.

"Ouch. That sounded like it hurt."

He turned to see Sunny standing there with her back to him. Still holding his aching head, he quickly got in bed and pulled the sheet over him. "You can turn around now."

She turned.

Corbin had been right. Sunny had been named appropriately. Her smile was almost as blinding as the sun.

"Good morning, big brother!"

Her loud greeting crashed through his sore, pounding head like marching band cymbals. He cringed and held up a hand.

"Softer, please."

Her smile got even brighter as she lowered her voice. "Looks like you must have stopped at the Hellhole after you left me and Corbin last night. I'm a little upset you didn't invite us along. Or say goodbye." She held up a to-go cup and bakery bag. "But I'm not one to hold a grudge. Coffee and a Cocoa Java Junkie muffin? Sheryl Ann said they were your favorite."

Just the thought of eating made his stomach churn. "No on the muffin. But I'd love that cup of coffee."

She walked over and handed it to him, her gaze drifting down to his lap. "Your man junk's showing."

"Shit!" He quickly grabbed the sheet to cover up and spilled coffee as he did. Thankfully, there was a lid on the cup, but the drops that hit his arm still burned like hell. "Sonofabitch!"

Sunny laughed. "You're a real mess, aren't you?"

He brushed the coffee off his arm and scowled. "I've had better days. How did you find me?"

"You buying Mrs. Fields' Boardinghouse is the talk of Butt Muffins."

"Butt Muffins?"

She hesitated. "When I was in high school, someone—not saying who—painted an extra *t* on the Nothin' But Muffins sign turning it into Nothin' Butt Muffins." Jesse laughed and she grinned. "It was pretty funny. At least, most folks thought so. Sheryl Ann not so much." She glanced around. "People are trying to figure out what you're going to do with this dilapidated building." She looked back at him. "What are you going to do with it?"

"Probably sell it for much less than I paid for it."

"So why did you buy it?"

"A whim."

She tipped her head and studied him. "Hmm? That's funny. From what Corbin has told me, you're not a whim kind of guy. He says you act all easygoing, but everything you do is calculated."

"Well, maybe Corbin doesn't know me like he thinks he does." Jesse certainly didn't know Corbin like he thought he did.

Sunny kicked off her flip-flops and sat down on the foot of the bed, crossing her legs in front of her like a teenager ready to share secrets. "Or maybe there's a reason you bought this place that you just don't want to tell me. I get it. You don't even know me. I'm just a stranger to you." She blinked her big brown eyes. "So why would you confide in little ol' me?"

It took a con artist to know one. "Oh, you're good," he said. "No wonder you have Corbin wrapped around your little finger. Just so you know, I'm not so easily manipulated."

Her bright smile returned. "Good to know. Corbin is an absolute pushover."

He frowned. "Which is how you got him to figure out a way to get the Holiday Ranch."

The surprise that entered her eyes was real. "If I had known what he was up to, I would have tried to stop him."

For some reason, he knew she wasn't lying. Probably because looking at her was like looking in a mirror. "But he's buying it for you. He told me it's where you want to live."

"At one time, it was. But I think a lot of girls dreamed about being one of the Holiday sisters. They were pretty and popular and had a ready-made clique. When you saw them in town all together, laughing and having such a great time, you couldn't help but want to be part of their sisterhood. I heard that they even had a club. A secret sister club. How awesome is that?"

When Jesse lifted an eyebrow, she laughed. "Maybe I was a little more infatuated with them than most girls. And I did draw a lot of pictures of their farmhouse with their amazing barn. But I was a young kid who craved a family and a permanent home." She looked at him. "From what Corbin has told me, I think you can understand that."

Jesse understood all too well. He also understood you couldn't change who you were or where you came from. "You'll never be able to replicate what the Holidays have, Sunny. That's not how life works."

"I realize that, but Corbin doesn't seem to." She glanced down at the bakery bag she'd set on the bed. "My favorite muffin is Strawberry Sweet Cakes. Of course, Uncle Dan never bought muffins. Most of his unemployment checks went for beer. Corbin was the one who bought them for me. He took on whatever odd jobs he could get so I would have warm winter coats and cool athletic shoes . . . and Strawberry Sweet Cakes muffins." She lifted her gaze. Tears brimmed in her soft brown eyes. "Because of that, I'd do anything for him—including go along with his crazy scheme of becoming a rancher. Because as much as Corbin says he's getting the ranch for me, I don't think that's the truth. I think he dreamed about being a Holiday more than I did."

Jesse had figured out the same thing last night

when he was only halfway through the bottle of Jack Daniel's. That's why he had finished the rest of the bottle. He realized he was in a no-win situation. He was stuck between wanting his brother to have the home he'd always dreamed of and wanting Liberty's family to keep their ranch. There was no way to give both people he loved what they wanted.

And he loved Corbin.

He also loved Liberty.

He had realized it the moment he had watched her walk away. It was like she had taken his heart with her and left nothing but a gaping hole in his chest. Which was why he had jumped in his truck and headed straight to the Hellhole to try to fill it.

But whiskey hadn't filled it. The emptiness was still there. He realized that it had been there long before he had met Liberty. She had just made him aware of it. He'd spent his entire life trying to fill it with his wheeling and dealing and traveling . . . and with women who he couldn't even remember. Then Liberty had come along and filled the empty space with her feistiness and her challenges.

Now that their relationship was over, he felt twice as empty.

He leaned back on the brass headboard and closed his eyes. "Dammit."

Sunny sighed. "I'm going to say that you being such a mess isn't just about Corbin foreclosing on the Holiday Ranch. It's Liberty, isn't it? You've fallen for her just like Corbin did."

Jesse didn't even try to deny it. "I've fallen alright. I feel like I've fallen from a twenty-story building and splattered on the sidewalk below."

"Well, that is a pickle, isn't it?" Sunny said. "You're in love with a woman your brother is stealing a ranch from. You can't get any more pickily than that. And I guess Liberty loves you too."

He opened his eyes. "Doubtful. Especially now that Corbin is taking her family's home."

"I don't know a lot about love, but I don't think that's how it works. You can't stop loving someone just because they do jerky things. If that were true, no one would stay together and Liberty would have walked away last night and not tried to punch your lights out." When his eyebrows popped up, she shrugged. "I was watching out the window. I couldn't hear exactly what y'all were saying, but I did get that you lied to her. Since she looked so surprised when I mentioned you were my brother, I figured you hadn't told her." She sent him a contrite look. "Sorry. If you had clued me in, I would have kept my big mouth shut."

He shook his head. "It's my fault. I should have told her sooner. It's just that I was worried she would think exactly what she does—that I'm in cahoots with Corbin and wanted to take her family's ranch all along."

"I can see why she'd think that. Especially when you and Corbin are business partners." She nibbled on her thumbnail. "What we need to do is figure out some way to convince her that it's not true."

"We?"

She blinked at him. "Yes, we. You're my brother. If I'm ever going to get you to trust me and confide in me and accept me as your little sister, I have to prove myself to you. And I figure the only way to do that is to get your woman back and that sad whipped puppy-dog look off your face."

Jesse scowled. "I don't have a whipped puppy-dog look."

"Then you haven't looked in the mirror. And since we look so much alike, it's kinda freaking me out. I hope I never look as pathetic."

"Gee, thanks."

She grinned. "You're welcome. Now, stop yakking and let me think." She nibbled on her thumbnail again. "The best way to prove your love to Liberty is to get her ranch back. Which means we need to convince Corbin that he really doesn't want the Holiday Ranch. And that won't be easy. When our brother sets his mind to something, he's like a dog with a bone. He won't let go until he decides to."

Even though Jesse's mind was sluggish and hungover, there was something about Sunny's words that struck a chord with him. "Until he decides to." He stared at her as a plan formed. "That's it!" He cringed when pain shot through his head.

"Softer, please," Sunny said with a smirk.

He sent her an annoyed look before he continued in a softer voice. "Corbin has never ranched before in his life, right?"

"Right. In fact, the one time we went horse

back riding in Colorado for one of my college spring breaks, he looked scared to death the entire time." She grinned slyly. "Of course, I didn't help matters when I slapped his horse on the rump and got it to take off with him at a full gallop."

Jesse laughed. "Why you little devil."

She smiled widely. "Just a little sisterly teasing. Believe me, you'll get your fair share."

Surprisingly, Jesse was looking forward to it. But first he had to get this mess untangled. "Obviously, Corbin doesn't have a clue about how hard ranching is. So we need to show him."

"What do you mean?" Sunny asked before her eyes widened. "Oh, I get it. If we can make him hate ranching, he'll sell the ranch to Rome."

"Exactly."

"But that isn't going to help the Holidays. They'll still be kicked out of their house."

"Not if we can talk Hank into showing Corbin the ropes—pardon my pun—of ranching. You and Corbin can move right into the house without evicting Hank, Darla, and Mimi. There are plenty of bedrooms now that their daughters are all gone. Once Corbin figures out how hard ranching is, y'all can leave and Rome will get the land and the Holidays will have their house to themselves again."

Sunny stared at him. "That's genius."

Jesse grinned. "Damn straight."

"Don't be getting a big head." She glanced around. "No genius would buy this rathole."

"For that comment, I just might have to turn this rathole into something profitable. But for now, we need to concentrate on our plan. And we can't tell Corbin."

"Of course, we can't. If he finds out we plotted against him, he'll work twice as hard at becoming a rancher just to prove us wrong."

"We're not plotting against him. We're merely helping him to see the error of his ways."

She flashed a smile. "I like the way you think, Jesse Cates." She jumped up. "So what are you waiting for? You need to work out our plan." Her eyes twinkled. "You might want to start by telling it to your woman. She's right down the street at Nothin' But Muffins."

Every muscle in Jesse's body tightened. "Liberty?"

Sunny rolled her eyes. "You got another woman?"

There would never be any other woman for him but Liberty. He was scared to death she might not forgive him. Even after she heard his plan. Something that must have been written all over his face.

"Now you listen up, Jesse James Cates." Sunny gave him a look that was pretty badass for a little redheaded gal who smiled all the time. "You either get up, get dressed, and get your butt down to Butt Muffins or I'm going down there and telling Liberty what a chickenshit my big brother is."

Chapter Nineteen

After a restless night of no sleep, Liberty got up the following morning and broke the news to her parents and Mimi that Jesse hadn't come through. Corbin was taking the ranch. Daddy cussed a blue streak, Mama just sat there looking sad, and Mimi refused to believe it.

"I'm not giving up on Jesse," she said. "He'll fix it. You just hide and watch."

Liberty had believed that too. She had put all her trust in Jesse. And he failed her. Last night, she'd been spitting mad at him. But after her temper cooled, she'd come to the realization that Jesse was only doing what she was doing: siding with his family.

"Jesse isn't going to fix this, Mimi," she said sadly. "Corbin is his family. We all know that family comes first."

Mimi gave her a stern look. "Family isn't just about blood, Libby Lou. Family is also about the folks who wiggle their way into our hearts without a trace of our blood. And I'd say we wiggled our way into Jesse's heart as much as he wiggled his way into ours."

Liberty couldn't argue the point. She knew Jesse cared about them.

Just not enough.

After talking to her parents and Mimi, she'd texted the sister loop and called an emergency Holiday Secret Sisterhood Zoom meeting. Because the ranch still didn't have Wi-Fi, she headed into town to Nothin' But Muffins. Thankfully, the morning rush had already left and the place was empty except for Sheryl Ann who was baking tomorrow's muffins in the back.

"So Jesse was in on everything from the get-go," Sweetie said as soon as Liberty had finished relaying everything to her sisters. "I can't believe it. He was so adamant about talking Corbin out of foreclosing on the ranch."

"Well, if he lied about Corbin being his brother—or half brother," Hallie said, "why wouldn't he lie about wanting us to keep the ranch?"

Last night, Liberty had thought the same thing, but that had been her temper talking. This morning, she was thinking more clearly.

"I know Jesse. And I know he didn't lie about wanting us to keep the ranch, Hal. But, just like we won't go against what our sisters really want, he won't go against what his sister wants."

"So where does that leave us?" Noelle asked. As usual she was in the kitchen of her pastry school, scooping batter into a pan. But today she looked different. Hallie figured it out before Liberty did.

"What the hell did you do to your hair, Elle?"

Noelle touched her short bob. "I got a bob. Isn't it the cutest? Luc talked me into it."

Hallie snorted. "Luc sounds more and more like an ignoramus because that haircut is not cute. It makes your face look like the Pillsbury Doughboy."

Noelle's eyes widened. "Did you just call me fat?"

"No, but you've always had a round face with chubby cheeks, Elle. A bob is the last thing you needed."

"Chubby! Did y'all hear that?"

"Enough, you two," Sweetie said. "We have a bigger problem to worry about. We need to convince Corbin to let Rome pay off the ranch."

"I don't think it's possible," Liberty said. "Believe me, Jesse is world class at convincing people to do things. If he couldn't, we can't. Especially when it sounds like Corbin is holding a grudge against our family for me breaking a date with him in high school—although he didn't see it as me breaking the date. He saw it as me trying to pull a twin switch on him."

"A twin switch?" Belle looked stunned. Liberty couldn't blame her. She had been just as shocked by Corbin's lie.

"I know. As if we would do that."

"You used to do it to us and Mama, Daddy, and Mimi all the time," Hallie said.

"That's different. You're family. Belle and I wouldn't do it to someone else. Especially a guy who had a crush on me."

"No, you'd just break a date with him," Sweetie said.

Liberty sighed. "You're right. I was wrong to break the date."

Hallie spoke up. "What is going on here? What happened to my tough, determined sister who is never wrong and never gives up and always keeps fighting?"

All her sisters stared back at her and she told the truth. "Maybe I'm just tired of fighting."

"That's not the Libby Lou I know."

The deeply spoken words came from behind her and the heart she'd thought was gone started beating twice as fast. She turned to see Jesse standing there looking like he'd been rode hard . . . and left out in a blizzard. His hair was more messed than usual. His eyes were bloodshot. His skin had a grayish tint.

Just the sight of him made her feel complete and utter joy . . . and pain.

"Can we talk?" he said.

She turned away—mostly because if she kept looking at him, she knew she'd give in to the strong pull he had over her. "There's nothing to say, Jesse. I know you're sorry. And I know you tried to talk Corbin into allowing Rome to pay off the loan. So let's just leave it at that." She tried to hold back the tears, but it was a losing battle.

Fortunately, she had her back to Jesse.

Unfortunately, she was facing her sisters.

"Libby." Belle's eyes welled with tears.

"Ahh, honey." Sweetie pressed a hand to her chest.

"Oh, Liberty." Cloe's voice quavered.

"What?" Noelle said. "Why is Liberty crying?"

"Wait a second." Hallie blurted out. "Is something going on with you and that jackass who helped his brother steal our ranch, Libby? Hey, asshole! Taking our ranch is one thing, but you hurt my sister and I'm going to hurt you."

"Hurting her is the last thing I want to do," Jesse said. He placed a hand on her shoulder and squeezed gently. "Please, Libby Lou, don't cry. Please just give me a chance to explain."

Try as she might, she couldn't ignore his plea. "I'll call y'all later," she said to her sisters before she closed her laptop and got up. Without saying a word to him, she headed for the door. Once they were outside, she whirled on him. "So say what you want to say."

He reached out and gently brushed a tear from her cheek. "Not here. I'll follow you out to the ranch."

"I don't think that's a good idea. Daddy will shoot first and ask questions later."

He studied her, his brown eyes sad and heartbreaking. "And you'd care?"

She wished she could lie, but her aching heart wouldn't let her. "I'd care."

She waited for him to return the sentiments, but he didn't. "Regardless of your daddy filling my hide with buckshot, I need to talk to your family." He hesitated. "Then we need to talk."

The way he said it didn't sound promising. It sounded like he was dreading whatever he had to say. Which could only mean one thing. He was going to tell her he was leaving.

Why she felt so hurt, she didn't know. Especially when she had already ended things with him. But she did feel hurt. Her heart felt like an egg that's fragile shell was slowly cracking. All the way back to the ranch, every time she glanced in the rearview mirror and saw him sitting behind the wheel of his ridiculous vehicle, those cracks got bigger and wider.

Like she had predicted, as soon as they pulled up in front of the house, her daddy came striding out of the barn looking fit to kill. He didn't have his shotgun, but he did have a pitchfork that he was pointing at Jesse.

"Get off my property, Jesse Cates! This ain't your ranch yet."

Jesse came around the front of the truck with his hands held high. "You're right, sir. But I'm not here to claim the ranch. I'm here to try and make sure it stays yours."

Hank lowered the pitchfork, as surprised as Liberty was. "So you're going against your own brother?"

"No, sir. I can't do that. When I invested in Corbin's business, I promised him that I wouldn't interfere and he'd always have free rein to run it the way he saw fit. Even if I disagree with his decisions, I won't go back on my word."

"Then how are you going to make sure my family keeps the ranch?" Liberty asked.

He flashed his cocky smile. A smile she had

missed way too much. "By giving Corbin exactly what he thinks he wants. Holiday Ranch. But my plan includes you being willing to allow him and our sister to move in here so you can show my greenhorn brother exactly how tough ranching is. Depending on how difficult you make it, I figure he'll be out of here within a month. Two, tops." He glanced at Liberty. "Then everything can go back to normal."

Normal. Why did she suddenly hate that word so much? Probably because she knew what normal was for Jesse. Traveling around and not having a care in the world.

The screen door flew open and Mimi stepped out to the porch with Mama right behind her. Both women had to be eavesdropping because they were smiling. When they came down the porch steps, they each gave Jesse a big hug.

Mimi sent Liberty a smug smile. "I told you our Jesse would fix things." She hooked an arm through Jesse's. "Now you come inside and I'll open that bottle of elderberry wine so we can celebrate."

Jesse shook his head. "We can't celebrate yet, Ms. Mimi. First, we have to get Corbin to agree to let y'all live here. And it has to be his idea."

"And how do you think we do that?" Daddy asked. Liberty was wondering the same thing. But it appeared Jesse had thought his plan through because he answered quickly.

"You invite Corbin to dinner before the eviction date and show him around, making sure you give him a long list of everything he needs to do to keep up the house and the gardens and the stock."

"But we don't have any stock," Mama said.

"I figure Rome can help you out with that." He grinned. "My job will be to put a bug in Corbin's ear about needing someone to show him the ropes of his new ranch."

Everyone stood there mulling over the plan for a few minutes before Daddy laughed. Liberty couldn't remember the last time she'd heard her daddy's big barrel-chested laugh. "Well, son, it sounds like you got things all figured out."

"I don't think we should count our chickens before they're hatched, sir. Corbin might not go for it. And even if he does, he could take to ranching better than I think."

"Well, at least we'll have tried," Mimi said. "That's all we can do. And I don't see why we can't go on in and have a glass of my wine just to celebrate a good plan."

"Can I take a rain check, Ms. Mimi?" Jesse glanced at Liberty. "I need to talk to Libby."

A big smile spread over Mimi's face and she patted his arm. "Of course you can. Libby Lou, why don't you take Jesse up to the hayloft where it's nice and cool and quiet."

Liberty knew what Jesse wanted to talk about. He was breaking things off with her. She knew he cared for her and her family, which was why he'd come up with the plan to save the ranch. But she also remembered too clearly the scared look on his face when she'd mentioned love.

This was confirmed when they got up into the

hayloft and he acted so nervous. He pulled off his hat and ran a hand through his hair, then put it back on before taking it off again and rolling the brim through his hands as he looked around.

"Nice loft."

"Is that what you want to talk to me about? How great my hayloft is?"

His gaze settled on her. "No."

"Then what?"

He cleared his throat. "I've done some thinking . . . and well . . . I—"

She tried to act like her heart wasn't cracking in two and cut him off. "Like I said before, you don't have to explain anything to me, Jesse. I didn't think this was forever. You've made it perfectly clear you don't do forever. That's okay. I don't know if I'd be real good at forever either. So you can leave and not feel guilty. I'll be just fine."

He studied her for a long, heartbreaking moment before he spoke. "You might be fine, Libby Lou, but I won't be." His eyes softened. "I love you. I've fought it for a long time and I just can't fight it anymore."

She blinked. "You fought it? Are you saying loving me is like catching a bad cold?"

"No." He paused. "Although love does kinda feel like that. It makes you achy and out of your head. And you do make me ache, Libby Lou, and feel out of my head." He cringed. "Shit. This has to be the worst declaration of love in the history of love declarations. The only excuse I have is that it's the first and only declaration I've ever made. And I'm standing here shaking in my boots, scared to death that you don't feel the same way and that I'm gonna leave Wilder with a bigger hole in my chest than when I came."

"So you're still leaving?"

"No! I mean I'm not if you don't want me to. If you want me to stay, I'll stay . . . forever, Libby."

Liberty had worked so hard at being the tough Holiday sister. The one who didn't crumble easily. But she crumbled then. Her knees gave out and she crumbled into a sobbing heap, tears falling much faster than she could blink them back. Suddenly, Jesse's arms were around her and he was pulling her into a hard chest that smelled of soothing campfires and cool summer nights.

"Lib. Baby. Please don't cry."

She swatted his chest and spoke through a tear-clogged throat. "I don't cry!"

He rubbed her back. "Of course you don't." He kissed the top of her head. "But if you ever feel like you need to cry, it's safe to cry with me, Libby Lou. I promise I won't tell a soul."

That was about the sweetest thing she had ever heard. She lifted her head and looked into his eyes. "You make me feel achy and out of my head too, Jesse Cates. But you also make me feel so much more. Until you showed up, I forgot how to live. I was just fighting my way through each day without enjoying it. You taught me how to slow down and enjoy life. Now I can't imagine that life without you."

He brushed a tear from her cheek. "That's good, darlin'. Because I can't imagine life without you either." He kissed her. It wasn't a heated passionate kiss. It was a soft, sweet one. And yet, it rocked her world more than any other kiss. Because this kiss was filled with all the emotions both of them struggled to express. When he drew back, they were both smiling. Although Liberty's logical brain didn't let her smile for long.

"So how are we going to do this? How are we going to share a life when I live in Houston and you live . . . all over."

He shrugged. "I don't know. I guess we'll have to figure out a place to live that works for both of us." He hesitated. "Like maybe Wilder."

"Wilder? You'd move here?"

"For you, Libby Lou, I'd move anywhere." He leaned in to kiss her, but she stopped him.

"Just to be clear, I'm still ticked about you not telling me Corbin is your brother."

He grinned. "I figured as much. I also figured that this won't be the last time you get ticked at me." He pulled her closer. "So I guess it's a good thing I'm excellent at making up for my sins."

He kissed her.

And he was right.

She forgot all about his sins . . . and wanted to do some sinning of her own.

Chapter Twenty

"Jesse, I swear I'm going to throw up if you don't take this blindfold off me."

Jesse glanced over at Liberty sitting on the truck seat right next to him and couldn't help grinning. Her eyes were covered with his bandana and her mouth was turned down in a mean-looking scowl.

"Hold on, darlin'. We're almost there." He took her chin and turned her face toward him so he could brush a kiss on her lips. The way she melted into the kiss, disrupted the fat pug sleeping on her lap. Buck Owens snuffled his annoyance and Jesse drew back to find the dog glared at him with buggy eyes.

Liberty blindly petted the dog. "See, even Buck is over it. Aren't you, baby?"

The pug sent Jesse a smug look and Jesse rolled his eyes. "I'm not sure how I ended up with a feisty dog and a feisty woman."

Liberty looked as smug as Buck. "Just lucky I guess."

He grinned. "I guess I am."

When the old mansion came into view, Jesse felt even luckier. There had always been something about the house that tugged on his heartstrings. Now he knew why.

The house had been put thorough a lot and was more than a little rough around the edges. But if you could look past the fake façade and the tarnished past, the house was sturdy and well built and had heart. With a little love and a lot of work, it was going to be something special.

Just like Jesse.

Because of his tarnished past, he had viewed himself as a dilapidated old house that didn't deserve love. Shirlene and Billy had tried to make him see his worth. But it had taken a sassy, dark-haired beauty who challenged him at every turn for him to realize that he *was* worth saving. He deserved to be loved. He deserved to be happy.

And damned if he wasn't.

The last couple weeks had been heaven on earth. Liberty had agreed to go back to Bramble with him to meet his family. If he hadn't known Liberty was right for him before, he figured it out in Bramble. She and his sisters, Mia and Adeline, took to each other like ducks to water. She wasn't starstruck by Mia's husband, Austin, who had played quarterback for the San Diego Chargers and Dallas Cowboys, and was now a sportscaster for Fox Network. She didn't flinch at Billy's brashness or blush at Brody's teasing or get shocked by Shirlene's bluntness.

His tough girl fit right in.

"I love your family," she'd whispered later that

night when they were tucked beneath the sheets of his childhood bed. "I'm glad you found them."

"I'm glad I found them too." He'd kissed the top of her head. "But I'm even more glad I found you."

She'd looked up at him with a wicked smile. "Care to prove it?"

He'd proven it.

In fact, he was going to prove it for the rest of his life.

He pulled into the circle drive in front the boardinghouse and jumped out. He smiled when he saw what the construction crew he'd hired had accomplished in just two weeks—of course, money talked and he was paying them double what they usually earned.

The crumbling columns had been replaced and the old ones stripped of old paint and vines before being repainted. The windows had been cleaned, panes replaced, and the trim painted a crisp white to match the columns and upstairs balcony railing. The front door had been sanded and painted a deep forest green and an engraved brass plate had been affixed to the center of it.

Jesse had ordered the plate himself. He hoped it would not only gain him points with Liberty, but also her sisters. Hank, Darla, and Mimi had accepted him, but the Holiday sisters were still skeptical of his and Liberty's relationship. Especially Belle. He had only talked to her once via Zoom, but he'd gotten the Don't-Mess-With-My-Sister vibe loud and clear.

Of course, Corbin wasn't real happy about

Jesse dating Liberty either. He hadn't tried to talk Jesse out of being with her—that wasn't Corbin's style—but his silence spoke louder than words. Jesse knew he was still holding a grudge against Liberty and her family, but Jesse figured he'd get over it soon enough. The Holidays were impossible to resist.

Especially since Corbin was going to be living with Hank, Darla, and Mimi.

His agreement to let the Holidays stay in the two-story farmhouse wasn't because of Hank listing everything that needed to be done on the ranch, or Darla's home cooking, or Jesse mentioning that any smart CEO always kept the previous employees of a purchased company on to help with the transition. It was because Sunny had fallen in love with Mimi and refused to kick her out of her house.

Corbin couldn't refuse Sunny anything. Although he'd only agreed to let them stay until the end of June.

Jesse would have thought Sunny's attachment to Mimi was all part of their plan if he hadn't seen the two women together. They had hit it off immediately. Mimi said it was because Sunny reminded her of herself.

"Jesse Cates!" Liberty hollered from the truck. "What the heck are you doing? Buck and I are burning up in this truck!"

Realizing he'd been woolgathering, he quickly reached into the truck and got Buck before he took Liberty's hand to help her out. "Sorry, darlin'. We're here." He took off the blindfold.

She blinked in the bright sunlight. "Don't you *sorry* me. It's one thing to blindfold someone in the privacy of a bedroom. It's quite another to blindfold them in broad daylight and drive them to Lord knows—" She stopped blinking and stared at the house before she glanced back at him. "Did you do this?"

"I wish I could say yes. I would have loved to be part of the transformation." He winked at her. "But it's hard to renovate a house and keep an extremely high-maintenance woman happy at the same time."

She swatted his arm. "I am not high maintenance."

"Of course you aren't, darlin'." He shifted Buck and held out his arm. "You want to go in, low-maintenance woman, and see the rest of the surprise or do you want to stay out here and yell at me?"

She shot him an annoyed look, but took his arm. Before they had even reached the door, she froze and stared at the engraved brass plate. "Holiday Bed and Breakfast?"

"I thought it had a better ring to it than Fanny Fields' Bed and Breakfast."

Her eyes were confused. "But I don't understand. I thought you didn't want to be the proprietor of a bed-and-breakfast."

"I thought a lot of things." He smiled. "But sometimes you just have to go with your gut. My gut says this is a good idea. The town of Wilder needs a place for folks to stay. And I was thinking . . . if Corbin won't let your family keep the ranch, we could always build ourselves a big red barn out back. It makes perfect sense to have one on the same property as yours and Belle's event-planning business." He hesitated. "And I figured since it was your idea, you'd might want to help me run it . . . when you're not planning events."

She stared at him. "But you don't know anything about running a bed-and-breakfast. Neither do I."

"True. But we didn't know anything about falling in love either. And look at us now." He gave her a quick kiss before he took two keys out of his pocket. Buck started wiggling with excitement thinking it was a treat and he set the dog down before he slipped his hand into the open collar of Liberty's shirt and dropped one key into her bra. "For safekeeping." Then he used the other to open the door.

Buck waddled in before them. Jesse slipped the key back in his pocket before he scooped up Liberty in his arms and carried her in.

"What are you doin', Jesse Cates?"

"Just going with my gut."

The foyer still looked as pathetic as it had before. Although the floor had been swept clean and there were no chunks of fallen ceiling he had to step over.

"It still needs a lot of work," he said as he carried her up the stairs. "But I think it's going to be something when we're finished. For now, all we need is a bedroom, bathroom, and kitchen."

She stared at him. "You want to live here?"

He set her down at the top of the stairs. "Did you have a better idea? Wouldn't it make sense that we have a place of our own?"

She opened her mouth, then closed it. Then opened it again. "Are you asking me to move in with you, Jesse Cates?"

He nodded. "That's exactly what I'm asking, Libby Lou. I want to wake up every morning and see your sleep-creased face and bed head." She swatted him and he laughed. "I do. I got used to waking up with you when we were in Bramble. But I don't think your daddy is gonna go for me moving into your bedroom with you. And now that Corbin and Sunny are moving in, there won't be enough room, anyway." He took her hand. "Now come on and I'll show you our room." He whistled for Buck who was still investigating the downstairs. "Come on, Buckaroo!"

Once the pug had joined them, he drew Liberty down the hallway to the only door that had been refinished. It was the same room they'd shared before. The corner room with all the windows. Except now, those windows had panes.

When he opened the door, it was like stepping onto a sunlit explosion of color. The walls were a deep blue and everything else—the comforter, pillows, upholstery, and curtains—was done in a variety of different bright colors.

As Liberty looked around in stunned shock, he explained. "I know you were thinking about naming each room after desserts, but since we're using the Holiday name, I figured we should name each room after a Holiday sister."

"And which sister's room is this one?"

He pulled her into his arms. "That's a good question, Libby Lou. It's not the Sweetheart Room because that will be done in shades of pink. The Clover Room will be done in greens. The Belle Room will be done in red, white, and blue. The Halloween Room in black and orange. The Noelle Room in red and green."

Liberty glanced around at all the color. "This is the Liberty Room? Shouldn't it be done in red, white, and blue too?"

Jesse shook his head. "Nope. Because three colors could never define you, Liberty Holiday. You're an explosive firework bursting into the night sky in a shower of color. You're loud, fiery, heart pounding, and breathtaking."

She slowly took the room in before she looked back at him. Tears glistened in her beautiful green eyes. He knew they were happy tears by the soft smile on her lips.

"I think I can live here with a cocky cowboy."

He grinned. "Well, that's real good, darlin', because my only other plan was living in Corbin's trailer or Bubba's truck."

She hooked her arms around his neck. "I wouldn't mind either. As long as I get to sleep on top."

Desire settled deep and low. He wanted to lead her right over to that big ol' bed and let her have complete control. But they had some unfinished business. "I'll make you a deal. You can be on top whenever you want, Libby Lou, if you win the next challenge."

"And what challenge would that be?"

He got down on one knee and pulled the ring box out of his pocket. "Spending the rest of your life with me." He opened the box and Buck came over to investigate. When he discovered it wasn't food, he waddled off to continue exploring the room. Jesse laughed before he glanced up at Liberty.

She looked stunned and beautiful. His heart swelled with love.

"That's a pretty big challenge," she whispered with tears glimmering in her eyes.

"Believe me, I know. I'm not easy to live with. But, then again, neither are you."

She scowled. "You really are bad at love declarations."

He grinned. "But you still love me." He was glad she didn't even hesitate to answer.

"I do, you ornery man."

"So what do you say, Libby Lou?" He took the ring out of the box. For his fiery girl, he had chosen an engagement ring with a large ruby in the center and diamonds encircling it. "You up for the challenge?"

She hesitated. "Are you? Even if I can't have kids?"

He got to his feet and looked into those beloved green eyes. "I don't care if you can or can't have kids, Liberty. What I care about is making you happy. If you don't want kids, we won't have kids. If you do, we will. Because if I've learned anything in my life it's that being able to have children doesn't make you a mama. Being willing to love a child with all your heart does."

She flung her arms around his neck and hugged him tight. "How did I find you, Jesse Cates?"

"I believe I found you, Lib." He drew back and held up the ring. "Now are you going to say yes?'"

"Yes! I accept the challenge of marrying you, Jesse Cates. And you know what?"

He slipped the ring on her finger before he pulled her back into his arms. "What, my love?"

She smiled the kind of smile he wanted to see every day for the rest of his life. "I think we're both gonna win this one."

He did too.

He damn well did too.

THE END

Turn the page for a Sneak Peek at the next Holiday Ranch romance!

Sneak Peek

Wrangling a Hot Summer Cowboy

Chapter One

It was an image straight out of a country dream.

Miles and miles of land stretched out for as far as the eye could see. Land filled with mesquite trees, scrub oak, late spring wildflowers, and early summer grasses. A herd of longhorn cattle lazily munched on those grasses, their tails occasionally lifting to flick at pesky insects. Or maybe just to fan their bodies in the sizzling May heat.

Amid the land and cattle sat a big red barn and quaint two-story farmhouse. The barn brought up images of six laughing girls—grooming thoroughbred horses and cuddling newborn kittens and jumping in shrieks of delight from the hayloft. The farmhouse with its wide porch brought up another image.

An image of a loving family.

As always, the image caused Corbin Whitlock to feel numerous things: pain, desire, envy, and anger. The anger always won out. It was a much easier emotion to deal with than the others.

"I don't know how in the hell I let you and Jesse talk me into allowing the Holidays to stay for a month, Sunshine Brook Whitlock," he grumbled as he maneuvered his truck around a pothole in the road. "I should have my head examined."

His sister smiled at him from the passenger seat. Sunny had been aptly named. She was brilliance and warmth and life giving.

She was certainly his life.

"I'm not going to argue that point, Corbin Conrad Whitlock," she said. "I have never understood the things that go on in your head."

"Just like I don't understand the things that go on in yours. Allowing the Holidays to stay for a month will only make it harder for them to leave." He took his eyes off the dirt road to give her a stern look. "And they are going to leave, Sunny. They aren't like all the stray animals you kept bringing home when we were kids."

Not that they had ever been able to keep any of those strays. Which probably explained why Corbin had grown so attached to Taylor Swift. He glanced down at the tiger-striped kitten curled up in his lap and gently stroked her soft, tiny head as he continued.

"The Holidays aren't strays. They have six daughters who I'm sure will be more than happy to take them in. Or at least four of them will."

Sunny laughed. "Don't tell me you're still holding a grudge against Liberty and Belle for that little high school prank they pulled. I've pulled worse pranks than that."

Sunny did have a prankster nature, but her jokes were all in good fun. Liberty and Belle's prank hadn't been fun. Not fun at all. When he didn't say anything, Sunny sighed.

"Okay. I guess my pranks never broke anyone's heart."

"Liberty didn't break my heart. You have to be in love with someone for them to break your heart and I was never in love with her."

"No, just infatuated. And since you're taking their family's ranch, I have to wonder if you weren't infatuated with the entire Holiday family."

He snorted. "Not hardly. Like I've told you and Jesse repeatedly. Foreclosing on this ranch isn't about the Holidays." He glanced at her. "I wanted you to have your dream home."

She opened her mouth as if to say something, but then closed it again and smiled brightly. "Thank you, big brother. You always have given me everything I've dreamed of. Now about that Lamborghini for my birthday?"

He looked back at the road. "Not a chance. After the way you were driving in Paris, I'm not about to buy you a fast car." He pulled in behind the U-Haul truck he'd been following to the ranch. "I ordered you a Subaru. They're supposed to be some of the safest cars on the road."

Sunny rolled her eyes as she reached for the door handle. "Whoopee. I just love playing it safe."

Corbin didn't find her sarcasm funny. Keeping Sunny safe was a full-time job. While he had always been cautious, she had always been adventurous and a daredevil. She never did anything illegal—besides driving way too fast—but she was always willing to try something new, exciting . . . and dangerous.

Against his wishes, she'd skydived, mountain climbed, and scuba dived with sharks. She'd driven Formula One racecars and motocross motorcycles and taken flying lessons. After graduating from college, she'd wanted to travel all over the world. He'd put his foot down and closed his wallet on that dream. But she *had* talked him into going to an art school in Paris.

Corbin had been worried sick the entire three years she'd been gone—even with the security team he'd hired to keep an eye on her.

But she was home now. Their home. And he could finally relax.

Although, as he climbed out of his truck, he didn't feel relaxed. A knot of unease, anxiety . . . and guilt settled in his stomach. It pissed him off. He had every right to be there. The Holidays had known what would happen if they failed to make the loan payments on the ranch. He wasn't at fault. He had only done what any smart businessman would do.

The Holidays would find another place to call home. In fact, at their age, they should probably be living in a retirement community. A ranch this size was too much for three old people to handle by themselves. The debt they got themselves into proved it.

But knowing that didn't stop his guilt from growing when Mitzy Holiday, or Mimi as everyone called her, came around the side of the house.

The Holidays' grandma looked like she had every other time he'd visited the ranch—like she'd been rolling around in the dirt. Her gardening gloves, T-shirt, jeans, and roper boots were covered in dark soil. There was even a smudge on her nose and the wide brim of her hat.

Completely unconcerned with the dirt, Sunny hurried over and gave her a tight hug. Sunny had fallen in love with Mimi after only one meeting. Which wasn't surprising given that Sunny seemed to love everyone . . . while Corbin only tolerated people.

And Sunny wasn't the only female in Corbin's life that had fallen in love with Mimi. Tay-Tay woke up from her slumber and took one look at the old woman and started struggling to be let down. But since there were way too many dangers on a ranch for a tiny kitten, Corbin kept a tight hold as Mimi walked over to greet Tay with an ear scratch.

"Hello, sweet girl." Mimi looked at Corbin. "It's a good thing you're moving in early. My arthritis tells me it's going to rain this afternoon. Which is why everyone is busy getting the ranch work done early."

Corbin didn't have a clue what ranch work she was talking about. His sister's pleas weren't the only reason he'd let the Holidays stay for a month. There were a lot of things Corbin didn't know about running a ranch. If her twinkling eyes were any indication, Sunny knew he didn't have a clue what Mimi was talking about and was thoroughly enjoying the fact.

"Then I guess we need to get these boxes unpacked so Corbin can help with that ranch work," she said with a smug smile. "After all, this is your ranch now, Cory."

He shot her an annoyed look before he headed over to the movers and started issuing orders about where he wanted them to put the boxes.

There weren't that many. He had to wonder why he'd even bothered to hire men to help them move. After moving so much when they were kids, he and Sunny had learned to travel light. Or possibly live light. Sunny had brought very little back with her from Europe. Since Corbin planned to keep the penthouse in Houston for when he traveled there on business, he had left all the furniture and household items. He would worry about buying more for the ranch once the Holidays had moved out. For now, he'd only brought clothes, books, personal items, and his office equipment. Not wanting the moving men to drop the box with his laptop and printer, he handed Tay-Tay to Sunny and grabbed it.

Darla Holiday was there to greet them when they stepped in the door.

"Corbin! Sunny! We're so happy you're here." She had always been nice and welcoming, but he struggled to reciprocate. With her dark hair and soft green eyes, she looked like Liberty and Belle. She glanced at the box he carried. "I bet you'll want that in the study."

He expected the study to be filled with family photographs and Hank's things, but it had been completely cleaned out.

As was the upstairs bedroom she showed him to next.

"We figured you'd want the room with the biggest bed." Darla plumped one of the pillows. "This was Liberty and Belle's room. We got them twin beds like the other girls, but they flat refused to sleep separately so we had to get them a queen. Which is ironic since they're twins."

Corbin didn't laugh. He wasn't happy sleeping in the twins' room. Not happy at all. But he couldn't say anything. Not when Sunny was standing there and he'd just gotten through telling her he wasn't still holding a grudge. So he only nodded as Darla directed Sunny to the room next door. When they were gone, he released a grumbled cuss and stroked Tay-Tay's head as he glanced around.

At least there were no pictures or high school mementos. Nothing to remind him of a time he'd just as soon forget.

Although there was a scent. A citrusy scent that wiggled its way into his nose and brought with it memories of emerald eyes and raven hair and a husky laugh that would make any young boy become infatuated.

But Corbin wasn't a young boy anymore. Lemony scents and a soft, husky laugh no longer made him feel lightheaded and dopey. As an attractive man who ran a successful business, he'd had his fair share of relationships. He'd discovered most women were interested in two things: his bank account and a wedding ring. He never divulged his worth and he never wanted to get married.

Witnessing his parents' bond in unholy matrimony had been more than enough for him.

That wasn't the case with Sunny. She didn't remember their parents' knock-down-drag-out fights and had forgiven them long ago for dumping their two kids on every relative willing to take them.

Corbin struggled with forgiveness.

And forgetting.

The movers arrived with his boxes and Tay's things. He had them place the cat condo next to the window so she could look out and her box of toys in the closet, but when they brought in the high-tech litter box he'd just bought, he shook his head.

"Take that down to the laundry room." He scooped up Tay-Tay. "I'll show you where it is."

Once it was set up in a corner of the laundry room, he placed Tay-Tay inside the domed compartment so she could do her business. The kitten peeked out the opening of the space-age-looking dome as if to say *WTF*.

He laughed. "I know it's weird looking, but—"

"That's putting it mildly. What in tarnation is that contraption?"

He glanced up to find Mimi standing in the doorway. Her gardening hat was missing and her fine white hair looked like a bedraggled feather duster.

"It's a self-cleaning litter box."

"Well, isn't that fancy." She stepped in to get a closer look. "Where does the cat poop go?"

"There's a drum that spins and sifts it out and it falls into the airtight tray at the bottom."

She shook her head. "The things folks think of." Tay-Tay jumped out of the litter box and greeted Mimi with loud meows. She picked up the cat and cuddled her close. The fact Tay didn't scratch or nip her proved how much she loved the old woman. The kitten had never been much of a cuddler—except with Corbin. And it had taken him weeks to earn the cat's trust.

"So you all moved in?" Mimi asked.

"Not yet. I figured I'd set up my office first. I have some emails I need to send."

She hesitated. "You do realize we don't have Wi-Fi, right?"

He stared at her in disbelief. Who didn't have Wi-Fi in this day and age?

Obviously, the Holidays.

"Liberty tried to get someone to come out and fix it," Mimi continued. "But getting fix-it folks to drive all the way out here isn't easy." She smiled. "But I think it was a blessing in disguise. If we'd had Wi-Fi, all Liberty would have done was work and she never would have fallen in love with your brother."

Corbin tried not to scowl. He wasn't at all thrilled about Liberty and Jesse falling in love. And it had nothing to do with any leftover feelings Corbin had for Liberty. He was worried about Jesse getting hurt. But his half-brother was smart. He was the one who had helped Corbin make most his money. Corbin figured Jesse would see Liberty's true colors eventually.

"Maybe taking a break from work will be a blessing for you too." Mimi broke into his thoughts. "Now that you own a ranch, you might as well enjoy it. Sunny already headed out to look around her new home."

The thought of Sunny getting lost on the big ranch—or worse hurt—had him immediately concerned.

"Where did she go?"

"She was headed to the barn last time I saw her. But there's no need to worry. We don't have any aggressive animals in the barn that will harm her. Just a horse, and I'm sure your sister is smart enough to not go riding in a thunderstorm."

Corbin panicked. That was exactly something his sister would do.

"I need to go check on her." He started to take Tay-Tay, but Mimi stopped him.

"Why don't you leave her? I promise to keep her safe."

Corbin might not trust the other Holidays as far as he could throw them, but as he looked into Mimi's direct eyes, he realized he trusted her. He nodded before he headed out the back door.

As soon as Corbin stepped outside, his concern for his sister grew. Mimi was right. The clear, blue skies of the morning had been covered with a layer of angry, dark clouds that rumbled with thunder. Halfway to the barn the sky opened up and a deluge of water rained down. By the time he got inside, he was drenched from head to toe. He took off his hat and shook the water from it as he glanced around.

He had been inside the big red barn on more than one occasion. His uncle had been the foreman for the Holiday Ranch when Corbin and Sunny had first come to live with him and he had brought them out to the ranch numerous times before Hank fired him for drinking on the job.

"Sunny!" he called.

The only answer was the rain hitting the roof and the flutter of wings. He glanced up to the rafters. A few doves perched there, their beady eyes staring down at him as if questioning his right to be there.

He unsnapped his soaked western shirt and stripped it off as he moved further into the barn. It smelled like fresh hay and manure. No doubt from the horse that poked his head out of one of the stalls. Corbin sighed in relief. At least, he didn't have to worry about Sunny being tossed off a run-away horse and breaking her neck.

He hung his hat and shirt on the stall door across from the horse. "Hey, there, big guy."

The horse eyeballed him before he tossed his head and showed his teeth.

Damn, those were big teeth.

As a kid, he'd dreamed of owning a horse and becoming a cowboy. His Aunt May had loved Clint Eastwood as much as she'd loved the Oxycodone her doctor had prescribed for her bad back. For the year and half he and Sunny had lived with her, he had become infatuated with Clint's spaghetti westerns and learning to ride a horse . . . while wearing a really cool poncho. When they came to Wilder, Corbin had hoped his dream would come true. But Uncle Dan had been fired before he could teach Corbin how to ride. Not that Uncle Dan would have ever gotten around to teaching him. Kids hadn't been his thing. He'd only agreed to let them live with him because he owed their daddy money.

Now, Corbin was a little leery of horses. He'd had a bad experience horseback riding and hadn't attempted to ride again. But if he was going to become a rancher, he needed to get over his fear.

He reached out to pet the horse when a loud whinny had him snatching his hand back. Except the whinny hadn't come from the horse in front of him. He turned toward the open doors just in time to see a wild-eyed horse come charging through the sheet of rain.

Corbin's heart almost jumped out of his chest.

Not only because of the charging beast . . . but also because of the stunning woman who rode it.

**Order
WRANGLING A
HOT SUMMER COWBOY today!
at**
www.katielanebooks.com

Also by Katie Lane

Be sure to check out all of Katie Lane's novels!
www.katielanebooks.com

Holiday Ranch Series
Wrangling a Texas Sweetheart
Wrangling a Lucky Cowboy
Wrangling a Texas Firecracker
Wrangling a Hot Summer Cowboy—coming in May

Kingman Ranch Series
Charming a Texas Beast
Charming a Knight in Cowboy Boots
Charming a Big Bad Texan
Charming a Fairytale Cowboy
Charming a Texas Prince
Charming a Christmas Texan
Charming a Cowboy King

Bad Boy Ranch Series:
Taming a Texas Bad Boy
Taming a Texas Rebel
Taming a Texas Charmer
Taming a Texas Heartbreaker
Taming a Texas Devil
Taming a Texas Rascal
Taming a Texas Tease
Taming a Texas Christmas Cowboy

Brides of Bliss Texas Series:
Spring Texas Bride
Summer Texas Bride
Autumn Texas Bride
Christmas Texas Bride

Tender Heart Texas Series:
Falling for Tender Heart
Falling Head Over Boots
Falling for a Texas Hellion
Falling for a Cowboy's Smile
Falling for a Christmas Cowboy

Deep in the Heart of Texas Series:
Going Cowboy Crazy
Make Mine a Bad Boy
Catch Me a Cowboy
Trouble in Texas
Flirting with Texas
A Match Made in Texas
The Last Cowboy in Texas
My Big Fat Texas Wedding

Overnight Billionaires Series:
A Billionaire Between the Sheets
A Billionaire After Dark
Waking up with a Billionaire

Hunk for the Holidays Series:
Hunk for the Holidays
Ring in the Holidays
Unwrapped

About the Author

KATIE LANE IS a firm believer that love conquers all and laughter is the best medicine. Which is why you'll find plenty of humor and happily-ever-afters in her contemporary and western contemporary romance novels. A USA Today Bestselling Author, she has written numerous series, including *Deep in the Heart of Texas, Hunk for the Holidays, Overnight Billionaires, Tender Heart Texas, The Brides of Bliss Texas, Bad Boy Ranch, Kingman Ranch,* and *Holiday Ranch*. Katie lives in Albuquerque, New Mexico, and when she's not writing, she enjoys reading, eating chocolate (dark, please), and snuggling with her high school sweetheart and cairn terrier, Roo.

For more on her writing life or just to chat, check out Katie here:
FACEBOOK
www.facebook.com/katielaneauthor
INSTAGRAM
www.instagram.com/katielanebooks.

And for more information on upcoming releases and great giveaways, be sure to sign up for her mailing list at www.katielanebooks.com!

Printed in Great Britain
by Amazon